PAUL

HAUNTINGS

THE GIRL IN BLUE

In a flash she saw the smile on the girl's face turn to a look of horror. Her hands went out as if to push Lorna back, just as she put a foot forward to descend the steps. It skidded over a patch of moss and Lorna lost her balance. She threw out her arms but there was nothing to grab to steady herself. She felt herself falling down, down, down.

Also in the HAUNTINGS series:

PAULINE HUNT

HAUNTINGS

THE GIRL IN BLUE

Hippo Books
Scholastic Publications Limited
London

Scholastic Publications Ltd,
10 Earlham Street, London WC2H 9RX, UK

Scholastic Inc,
730 Broadway, New York, NY 10003, USA

Scholastic Tab Publications Ltd,
123 Newkirk Road, Richmond Hill,
Ontario L4C 3G5, Canada

Ashton Scholastic Pty Ltd,
P O Box 579, Gosford, New South Wales,
Australia

Ashton Scholastic Ltd,
165 Marua Road, Panmure, Auckland 6,
New Zealand

Text copyright © Pauline Hunt, 1990

First published by Scholastic Publications Ltd, 1990

ISBN 0 590 76302 4

Made and printed by Cox & Wyman Ltd, Reading, Berks
Typeset by AKM Associates (UK) Ltd, Southall, London

10 9 8 7 6 5 4 3 2 1

Chapter One

"Earth to earth, ashes to ashes, dust to dust . . ."
Lorna was surprised how little she felt. She had been
frightened in case she made a scene. Instead she
clutched her coat about her in that windswept
churchyard, numb and detached.

The vicar's monotone, the knot of people huddled
around the grave . . . This scene had nothing to do
with Gran. She could feel the force of her grandmother's dark brown eyes bearing down on her. She
glanced sideways at her mother who was mopping
away a tear with her handkerchief. She looked at the
high-heeled shoes and the lipstick, seeing them with
Gran's disapproving eyes.

Lorna's gaze left the small band of mourners
standing bleakly together on that wild and wet
January day and strayed down to the valley below.
Down over the moorland, past the wide, grey ribbon
of the reservoir into the valley dominated by the great
rectangular slabs of the cotton mills, sliced into tier

upon tier of identical windows so that they looked like gigantic blocks of chocolate set upon their sides. Tall chimneys pierced the black and smokey scene at irregular intervals.

She stared at the shiny slate roofs of hundreds of identical terraced houses crammed tightly round the glass-eyed mills. One of those was the home she and her mother shared.

Lorna had gazed down upon this scene so many times from the windows of Gran's cottage in the hillside village which was so much older than the valley town. Gran would recall how as a young girl she had watched the town mushroom across the valley when this spot was chosen for the railway carriage works.

A squeeze upon her arm brought Lorna back to the present. Instinctively she drew back, resenting the intimacy of her mother's touch. Her mother and her father's mother had never really been close. Not the way she and Gran had been.

Now her grandmother had been laid to rest by the side of her husband and her only son. It was all over. Lorna's mother's arm guided her out of the church-yard, away from the solid stone building where Gran had been baptized, married, held her son at his christening and where she now lay buried alongside her family.

The little knot of people trailed slowly across the village to the small stone cottage where Gran had lived.

The door was open. Lorna was startled to see things set out as for a party. Plates of sandwiches, drink, a fire blazing away – and Gran so careful about her rations and her coal.

Lorna could never remember seeing these people

setting foot in Gran's cottage before. And now here was old Mr Dean sipping a glass of something and recollecting "Emily and I started elementary school on the same day."

It wasn't Gran's way to entertain. She always kept herself to herself. Only Lorna had shared that fireside with her grandmother, watching the old woman knit. Sometimes they would listen to the wireless. At other times Gran would reminisce.

Lorna heard her mother's voice speaking in low, sympathetic tones. The vicar was saying something soothing to her.

"I know it hasn't been easy for either of you since your husband died." His voice was resonantly reassuring.

Something tugged at Lorna's inside as she saw her mother's eyes mist over. "It is such a pity she wasn't able to live to see the end of this terrible war."

She slid away. She had had enough. It was all wrong. An intrusion. Unobserved she let herself out of the back door of the cottage. Only Gran's dog heard the squeak of the latch as she opened the garden gate. Lorna swept the mongrel up in her arms, glad of his company. For the first time she felt the tears stream uncontrollably down her cheeks. Her body was convulsed by waves of grief as she ran against the biting wind.

"Gran. Gran. Don't leave me!" The wind carried away her cry. It stung her cheeks. This was real. This wild, lonely hillside where she always felt close to her father. And now Gran.

The moorland grass was springy, almost sharp, underfoot. It was scattered with small, jagged stones. Water squelched inside her shoes.

Her family, the family of her father and grand-mother, belonged to this uncompromising moorland, not to the shabby black town. It was here, she knew, that Mark had been in his element. Gran's young, long-lost brother who had become for Lorna the brother she had never had. Here he became a real companion.

Lorna tried racing him to the top of the hill. He always won. But that pleased her. Mark was strong and protective. There was nothing he did not do well.

She leaned, panting, on the strange, stumpy little tower that stood on the hilltop, breaking the skyline and acting as a beacon for miles around.

Now, for the first time since Gran had died, she realized just how different her own life was going to be. No more weekends with Gran while her mother went to look after her own mother. Strangely enough, that grandmother had always been the sickly one. Now, for the first time, she would not belong to the village any more. There would be no reason to visit, no house to welcome her. She was Gran's only relative. Unless . . .

What she had lost was more than just a loving grandmother. It was the end of the family to which she belonged. No one would ever again tell her stories of her father as a little boy or relate the exploits of the ambitious Mark, his daring and his poaching.

Lorna's eyes travelled a little way down the hillside to the ruins of the great house where Mark had risen from gardening boy to manager of the estate. The gardens he had designed there lay deserted, entangled with weeds.

"I told him never to write!" Lorna could still hear the ferocity of her grandmother's mysterious com-mand. Where, oh where was Mark now? Perhaps somewhere in the world he was going about his ordinary tasks, utterly unaware of today's sad ceremony.

Lorna stood alone on the hilltop, muffled against the elements, willing Mark with all her might to return home.

Chapter Two

Immediately she opened their front door Barbara Rawlinson saw that Lorna had put a match to the fire on her return from school and promptly forgotten all about it. The room was cold and unwelcoming.

Quickly she tossed off her coat and shoes and tried to coax the half-hearted embers back into some life. "Lorna!" She could at least smell sausages cooking, which meant that Lorna hadn't forgotten everything.

Normally she would have felt exasperated. It was bad enough cleaning the grate and setting the fire all ready to light before she went off to work in the morning – without having to do it all over again when she came home tired. But tonight she had her mind on other matters.

She glanced around the room, looking at it with the eyes of an outsider. The damp marks were beginning to show again where she had distempered the wall, but on the whole it didn't look too bad. At least it was tidy.

Lorna had drawn the blinds. If only the fire would take a hold the room would begin to look cheerful. Mrs Rawlinson stood up and glanced at herself in the mirror. The gas mantles gave a poor light. Dark shadows cast by the newly revived flames of the fire made her undoubtedly pretty face look drawn. Just lately she felt her age had begun to show.

In the kitchen it was obvious that Lorna had only just put the sausages in the frying pan. They wouldn't be ready for quite some time.

She wondered whether Lorna had been trying on her old dance dresses again. The girl loved to dress up and daydream when she was on her own. She thought her mother didn't know. But Mrs Rawlinson often noticed that the once glamorous dresses had been pushed back into her wardrobe in different places. She thought it wiser not to comment. Sometimes there were smudges of lipstick on Lorna's face which she had not properly washed off.

She ached for her daughter. Lorna had all the dark features and heaviness of her father's family. She wasn't a pretty girl. Her thick, wiry hair was uncontrollable, her body too strong and square to be graceful.

"I'm glad you managed to get some sausages." Barbara Rawlinson set about laying the table.

"I had to queue for ages and then he gave me a little parcel wrapped up for you." People, Lorna had noticed, were inclined to do favours for her mother.

"That's good." Mrs Rawlinson lit a cigarette as she waited for the sausages to cook. "I've got someone coming from work tonight who might be able to help us move Gran's furniture."

"Will be we able to get it here soon?" She saw her daughter's face light up immediately. She could not

7

understand Lorna's attachment to Gran's shabby old-fashioned furniture. She herself much preferred lighter, modern things.

Still, she had promised the girl she could have the huge chest of drawers. She could not say no. Particularly after standing firm about Patch. They could not possibly have a dog, living as they did in a small terraced house with no more than a backyard. Not only that: they were both out all day.

Lorna had protested persistently. Her mother had heard her weeping at night. It hurt but there was nothing she could do about it. Old Mr Dean had taken in the dog and said Lorna could go whenever she wanted to take him out for walks.

"We'll bring the chest of drawers here?"

Mrs Rawlinson was tired. It was hard enough coping on her own. She hadn't enough emotional energy to argue about everything. There wasn't a corner in Lorna's room to put the chest but she was too drained to take issue.

One thing old Mrs Rawlinson had always stipulated was that she would like Lorna to keep the wooden casket which held her few valuables. It contained nothing really precious, just a few old family keepsakes, like the enamel-painted cross she often wore.

Neither mother nor daughter knew exactly what was in the casket. Gran had kept it locked and so far they hadn't sorted out all the keys in the cottage. Lorna longed to investigate.

"Do you think you could get changed for when Doug comes round?" Mrs Rawlinson inquired apprehensively. Lorna looked up sharply at the familiarity of the name. She had never heard of him before.

"I haven't time." She disdained to ask who the man might be. She spread out her books on the living room table. "I've a lot of homework to do."

Barbara Rawlinson looked as though she wanted to say something. Instead she lit another cigarette. It was the first time anyone from work had called at the house. She wanted to create a good impression. She plumped up the cushions vigorously to dispel her irritation.

Chapter Three

It was obvious that Doug has spruced himself up for this visit. So much so that his well-greased hair shone like a mirror, his parting so straight and clear you could have drawn it with a ruler. The creases in his trousers were razor-sharp and his brightly coloured tie echoed his bouncy self-confident manner.

Lorna chose to ignore the friendly appeal of his eyes as he gripped her hand warmly in greeting. Doug looked round the room determined to praise.

"You've a lot of pictures," he commented, pausing in front of an oil painting of Mrs Rawlinson playing with her small daughter in the sandpit of their old home.

It showed a young, beautiful woman with golden hair laughing beside the dark-eyed serious little girl.

"Is this you?" he asked uncertainly.

Lorna's mother nodded. "My husband painted a great deal. Just for pleasure. He wouldn't put them on show. It wasn't until after he died," Mrs

Rawlinson paused, "that an uncle of mine framed them for us."

She looked flustered. "Can I get you something to eat?" she inquired, accepting the cigarette he was holding out to her.

"No thanks, we've just finished our tea. We always have a proper meal at night. Andrew needs it while he is growing so fast." His voice registered a father's pride.

Lorna felt an unexplained wave of relief. The man was obviously married.

Doug didn't seem to feel there would be any problem borrowing a firm's van one Saturday. Being transport manager meant he could wangle a bit of extra petrol. Lorna listened to his voice, slightly high, discordant and so self-assured. Why, she wondered coldly, if he was as capable as he suggested was he not away fighting in the Army like most people's fathers?

She wished her mother did not look quite so grateful. Admiring almost. Did she really have to flutter her eyelids so often? Lorna could easily have retreated to her room but something compelled her not to leave her mother alone with this man.

Doug seemed to revel in his appreciative audience. The details of the furniture moving exercise settled upon, he expanded on his responsibilities at work, the difficulty of getting reliable men . . . That was one of the problems in wartime.

Lorna, surveying their silhouettes etched by the firelight, realized it was the first time she had seen a man sitting in an armchair opposite her mother in the four years since her father had died. The contrast between the two men struck her forcibly.

Ralph Rawlinson would never have sat chatting like that. He was an altogether different sort of man.

Quiet, disconcertingly so at times. So quiet that his wife used to chide him for being unsociable, for intimidating their callers. People stopped dropping in. He was the sort of man who spoke if he had something to say, and only then.

Lorna remembered her father as a gentle, very determined man. Nobody could coerce him into doing something against his will. It was equally hard to make him angry.

Already this man was offering to mend the blocked high guttering which made the rain splutter against the kitchen window.

"Do you collect stamps?" Doug tried to engage Lorna in conversation when her mother went off to make a cup of tea. "We get quite a lot of foreign letters at work."

Lorna was not going to be drawn. "No," she answered shortly, putting her head down over her books.

It was late when Doug took his leave, arranging to bring a van round the following Saturday week. As he stood at the door Lorna head him say something about a singer at the Mechanics' Institute on Friday night. Would Barbara like to go? There would be a crowd of people there.

Her mother sounded wistful and uncertain. "I'll see," she murmured. Lorna knew very well what the problem was. Her mother had never gone out in the evenings and left her on her own.

Now, with no Gran for Lorna to visit, it would be even harder for Mrs Rawlinson to get out.

"Well T.T.F.N.," said Doug cheerfully. Lorna winced. She hated those wireless catch phrases. "Let me know about Friday," were his departing words.

Chapter Four

Mrs Rawlinson hardly noticed the cold in the kitchen as she filled their hot water bottles. She felt more light-hearted than she had done in years.

The last four years had been hard. She had tried her best. She wanted to give Lorna the stability she needed after the death of her much cherished father – and then the loss of Gran. But now she longed for a little fun for herself. If only Lorna were not so obviously disapproving of Doug.

Barbara Rawlinson had often felt that unspoken criticism before.

Her husband had been just the same when she sat chuckling at a foolish variety programme on the wireless. He had no time for light entertainment. Perhaps it was that he so often experienced pain, that he sensed his life would be too short to waste on things that were not important to him.

She had tried hard to share his interest in serious music and wildlife on the moorside. She had sat and listened to concerts and joined him on long walks. But it had not come easily to her. After all she had never pretended to be clever.

She had always left her mother-in-law's home with the feeling that she was an outsider, sensing that Ralph's mother did not approve of her make-up, her cigarettes or the fashionable clothes she made herself. Now Lorna was just the same.

Mrs Rawlinson clutched the hot water bottles under her arm. At thirty-four she longed to go out dancing while she still had the chance. Other people seemed to like her for what she was. If only Lorna would stay in by herself. After all she was nearly fourteen.

But still . . . She took a grip on herself. "Don't you think it's good that we'll get something done about the furniture?" she said brightly as Lorna came into the kitchen.

"Mmn." Lorna was non-committal. "Why is he not in the Forces?" she asked bluntly.

"He was wounded and sent home," her mother answered. "When he got back he found his wife had taken up with another man. He told her to go and took his son back to his mother's."

Lorna froze. The words had all the import of a siren warning of the approaching enemy.

Upstairs she placed the hot water bottle halfway down her ice-cold bed before standing in front of the bedroom window in the darkened room. She had the bigger of the two rooms, the one that looked up towards the Pike. The moonlight illuminated the little tower at the top of the hill.

Lorna sensed where the village of Pikeleigh lay nestling on the hillside, even though the blackout restrictions made it impossible to detect any lights or shapes in the darkness.

She felt her spirit go out to the village to which her father and Gran belonged, to the hillside of her family. To Mark.

Her eyes travelled up into the night sky. A solitary star was shining right above the tower. It was her star. She stared at it pleadingly, imploring it to soothe away the dull pain within her.

First Gran's death. Now this awful pushy man. She felt him threatening her. Even when she pulled the cold sheets over her head Lorna could not rid herself of the aching sensation that all the things she really cared about were being taken away from her.

As her consciousness began to ebb, she caught a glimpse of her fantasy brother, Mark, racing across the moorland. Oh how she needed him! She ran after him, reaching out for his strength and support.

Chapter Five

It was one of those leaden February days when people go outdoors only if they have to – and then dart speedily about their business. Lorna and her mother set out on the two-mile walk to Gran's cottage, their coats tightly belted against the gusts of blustering wind which only just managed to keep the heavy rain clouds at bay.

Mrs Rawlinson carried a shopping bag with a snack lunch. They were off to the cottage to spend the day stripping and cleaning, ready for the furniture removal. Turning out all Gran's possessions was a task from which Lorna recoiled. She loved everything exactly as it was.

Her mother was quiet as they walked briskly along the road of brick terraced houses all of the same 1890 vintage. No front gardens, just a step on to the street. One or two houseproud women were down on their knees whitening this step vigorously. Mrs Rawlinson nodded to them.

They walked silently up to the roundabout where all the main roads of Gauntsford met, passed the grime-covered Railway Tavern, then mother and daughter turned off into the road which led steeply up the hillside.

This was the route Lorna took every morning to school. She glanced up with a warm sense of pride as they passed her grammar school. Now they were coming to the smarter end of Gauntsford. Here were prosperous semi-detached houses with deep front gardens and names like Derwentwater and Moorside.

Soon these too where behind them and they were out in the open countryside.

Lorna's mood lightened a little. She picked up a stone from the pathway and tossed it ahead. She sensed Mark walking along with them and tried to see who could toss the pebble farther, running ahead to find small stones and hurling them as far as the wind would allow her. She was winning. She laughed.

They were nearly up to the reservoir. There it was, dull and pewter-like, reflecting the heavy skies. The stone cottage stood all on its own, near to the water's edge. Lorna always stopped at this point. It used to hurt whenever she looked at the cottage.

But time had begun to heal. She could accept that it was theirs no longer, the house that had been her only home until her father had died so suddenly one sunny day in November. Lorna would never forget the brightness of that day, the beauty of the red-gold autumn leaves. The outward world had shown no sign of the tragedy taking place within their home.

Now the new water company manager was installed there with his family. Barbara Rawlinson had found a small terraced house to rent within walking distance of the factory job she had taken.

Lorna turned to look at her mother, now quite some way behind. Her step was determined but heavy. She saw her turn to look at the cottage and glance away. Her slight figure looked defenceless. Lorna felt a pang of guilt. Why, oh why, could she not be nicer to her mother?

As Mrs Rawlinson had been ironing and listening to the wireless the night before, Lorna knew that she longed to be at the Mechanics' Institute social. She knew she should have offered to stay in alone. She was not frightened. It was a long time since her father had died. But not Doug. Not him!

It wasn't a pleasant task clearing Gran's cottage. Things looked sad and shabby. Gran had never thrown anything away, not even her son's school-books.

Lorna fought over parting with anything personal. She had just returned from delivering a parcel of old, carefully mended clothes to the vicarage – to be distributed to the needy – when a paper tossed up by the wind caught her attention. A pile of rough sketches lay waiting to be taken away by the salvage men.

Lorna examined them.

"I've just cleared those out!" Mrs Rawlinson sounded exasperated.

"But they're Dad's."

"I know, but we can't keep everything. They're just rough sketches. We've got the paintings."

"I'll keep them in my room out of the way. I'll look after them. Please don't throw them away."

Worn down by Lorna's endless arguments in favour of keeping everything, Mrs Rawlinson relented. Lora carefully tied up the pieces of paper ready to take home.

She slipped upstairs to Gran's room while her mother emptied the contents of yet another cupboard. There was the massive chest of drawers which was to be hers, the wood gleaming and rich with years of careful polishing.

Lorna ran her hands gently over the surface. She loved this huge chest with its antique carved handles. As her fingers travelled over the wood, they hit upon a little groove just above the top drawer. She tugged. To her amazement out slid a flat wooden surface covered with darkened leather like a writing table. Her own private desk! No one else would know about it. Lorna delighted in the secret aspects of her life.

Gently she eased it back. But something was catching. Lorna opened the drawer beneath. A sheet of newspaper had wedged itself at the back of the shelf. She tugged at it. The paper came away in her hand and the drawer slid easily back into place.

Everywhere in Gran's house there were old sheets of newspaper. Unlike most of them, this one had been carefully cut out. As her eye drifted casually over the yellowing page with its long columns of tightly packed type and tiers of uninviting headlines, her attention was instinctively seized by a familiar name. Wolstenholme. Gran's maiden name. She was riveted.

"Police are inquiring into the disappearance of Mr Mark Wolstenholme, who was estate manager at the Lodge until his departure last week. They wish to interview him in connection with the disappearance of a hundred gold sovereigns belonging to Mr Henry Judd.

Mr Judd, owner of the Lodge and one of Gauntsford's most prominent mill-owners, employed

Mr Wolstenholme (23) until he left suddenly last week following a disagreement.

Miss Emily Wolstenholme, sister of Mr Wolstenholme, with whom he lived at Greenways Cottage in Pikeleigh, told the *Chronicle* that she had no idea of the whereabouts of her brother. 'He left home to find a job,' she said. 'He has not been in touch since.' "

Lorna was transfixed. It sounded ominous and blackening. Mark steal? Impossible, she told herself. Nevertheless Gran's strange remark – "I told him never to write" – kept ringing through her head.

There must be an explanation. Gran had told her how Mark had walked off into the night with just a small bundle of clothes. He would never have taken the money. He wasn't like that. And Gran so honest she would never owe tradesmen a penny.

But a doubt lingered. Would someone who pinched rabbits also take sovereigns? Could he have borrowed the money, hoping to return it before the loss was discovered?

"Look at this, Mum!" Lorna called out as she charged downstairs.

Mrs Rawlinson read the part of the paper to which her daughter was pointing.

"No one ever said anything to me about it." There was an edge to her voice. "But then I don't suppose they would. To think all the time . . ." Her voice trailed away. "They were so close and proud."

Lorna was shaken. Her hero tarnished? The brilliant, all-powerful Mark. It couldn't be true. Gran didn't believe it. Of that she was sure. She had always spoken of her brother in warm, affectionate tones.

But where were those sovereigns now? It felt horrid to have your family under suspicion – and there was no one now to defend them. What did other people in the village know? Old Mr Dean? Did he suspect there was a thief in her family? An involuntary shudder passed through Lorna's body. Suddenly the village did not seem such a friendly place.

For the first time she was glad to go back with her mother to the anonymity of Gauntsford.

Chapter Six

"Mark didn't do it," Lorna thought fiercely as she propped herself up in bed, two cardigans over her pyjamas, the hot water bottle pressed between her knees.

She knew very well what it was like to experience unfair suspicion. She still smarted at the memory of being summoned before the headmistress, assumed to be the culprit who had sprinkled itching powder on a teacher's neck.

She knew who had done it though she couldn't say – a girl with a silky voice and assured manner whom all the teachers held in high regard. The sort of girl always asked to read aloud at prayers. Not like Lorna, so awkward and tactless.

She felt for Mark in his disgrace. Now she longed to find the sovereigns to prove his innocence. But how? It had all happened so long ago.

Lorna turned her attention to the pile of torn, yellow and dusty drawings she had retrieved from the cottage. She spread them out over her eiderdown.

She recognized familiar scenes of hillside and moorland. She lingered over the pencil drawing of the reservoir house, the home where she had spent her early years.

Lorna saw a picture of her father in her mind's eye, sketching on his drawing pad as she played around the hillside. With a sense of consternation she realized that time was beginning to blur the details.

It was his eyes, dark and solemn, she remembered best. Them and his voice, strong and uncompromising as its hard northern "a"s. Ralph Rawlinson's face had often worn the drawn look of someone for whom daily life was a physical struggle against ill-health.

When he died that November day Lorna had sensed that no one would ever love her so completely, accepting and taking pride in her for what she was. A dull ache now tugged at her stomach, the feeling she always experienced when she thought about her father.

Deliberately she turned her attention to the other pictures. Some were quite different in style. Much more meticulous, many of them concentrated on the big house and its gardens. These were intricate plans and sketches of flowerbeds, labelled with the proper botanical names in a strange, looping handwriting.

These were not her father's work. His handwriting was distinctive – and this was not his. She stared at them puzzled. Then with the thrill of sudden comprehension, she realized that these were drawings Mark had made in his days at the Lodge.

They were sketches setting out his ideas as he was designing and laying out the gardens. They showed how the imposing house must have looked in its

23

heyday, when carriages used to roll up for the weekend parties.

Here too was the sham castle sitting on the edge of the reservoir with the chimneys of Gauntsford in the distance. Henry Judd, at the height of his power, mill-owner dominating the valley, had decreed that they needed a ruined castle to make the view from the big house more romantic. Years later Lorna had often enjoyed clambering over its now deserted walls.

You could stand on those walls and on a clear day catch a glimpse of the Irish Sea, the sea across which Mark had sailed on his way to start a new life.

But however much the weeds now strangled the once magnificent gardens Lorna knew that his spirit could never be erased from the grounds where he had planted his ideas in the unyielding hillside.

Gran had often told her how, after working long hours on the estate, he would still be poring over books late at night, engraving the proper names of plants in his memory, familiarizing himself with their likes and dislikes.

He had been popular with the Judds, rising rapidly in power and influence. Lorna knew that he could do no wrong in their eyes – until the day he stepped beyond the boundaries of his position. His offence was to fall in love with the only daughter of the family. As she did with him. That was asking altogether too much for a humble working boy. He was banished from the estate.

Lorna wondered if someone else, jealous of Mark's success and popularity with the Judds, had seized advantage of his sudden dismissal to steal the money from the Lodge.

The story, she knew, had an unhappy ending. Not long after Mark had left, the Judds' daughter had died tragically in an accident. Heartbroken, her parents had moved away, never to return. The house and gardens were deserted. Gradually the buildings began to crumble and the natural wilderness of the moorland stole over the gardens.

Lorna pored over the sketches of Mark's gardens. She would search the grounds for his plants. She would rescue them from the weeds. Only she was left to care about this wronged man.

Chapter Seven

It was good to have a capable man around the place, Mrs Rawlinson thought gratefully as they stacked the van with her mother-in-law's possessions. Doug had simply taken charge, smoothing over difficulties, knowing how to dismantle the large wardrobe to get it out of the house, tackling practical tasks in a business-like way.

With his son Andrew he was busy lifting and carrying furniture, with cheerful, light music playing in the background. It was the first time she had met Andrew. He was a small boy with well-formed features outlined by a mass of wiry blond hair. But so untidy! That had come as a surprise because Doug was so fastidious about his appearance.

The lad's unkempt look obviously embarrassed his father. "Andrew's shirt never seems to stay inside his trousers," he said, trying vainly to tidy up his son's clothes. There was a sullen expression on the boy's face. He hardly ever smiled. Still, he was very good at moving the furniture. He worked with his father quietly and without complaint.

She and Doug kept bumping into one another as they carried things out of the cottage. "After you, Cecil," he would say, mimicking the wireless programme. "After you, Claude," she rejoined. He made her laugh. And that felt good.

Lorna had disappeared. Mrs Rawlinson assumed she had taken Patch for a walk. On the whole it was easier when she was out of the way. She tugged her mother's loyalties in opposition to Doug.

She wished he had not commented on how badly Gran's shelves had been fitted. Mother and daughter both knew they were the work of Lorna's father. He had never been handy at ordinary domestic tasks, however hard he tried. A look of hostility had flashed across Lorna's face and she had left the cottage without a word.

Mrs Rawlinson sank into a chair, relieved that for the first time in years she wasn't responsible for everything. She liked having Doug around.

Of course he wasn't clever like her husband. She knew that very well. But then he didn't leave her feeling inferior either. "Someone has read an awful lot of serious books," he had commented, looking at the shelves of the Princess Street living room. Nearly all had belonged to Ralph.

It was not that Barbara Rawlinson ever doubted her husband's devotion, but neither could she rid herself of the feeling that he wanted her to be something better. With Doug she felt completely natural and at ease. If only Lorna could like him.

There were times when she felt that her daughter was quite foreign to her, certainly far removed from the dainty, feminine little girl of whom she had

27

dreamed. It was hard to reach out to Lorna in her lonely and proud independence. If only she did not spend so much time wandering around the hillside or steeping herself in the past.

The intense love she felt for her daughter meant that it hurt to see her suffering. She so longed for Lorna to be happy. But the Rawlinson family did not seem made for laughter and fun, she thought, as she rose rather wearily out of her chair ready to return to the work in hand. Her husband and her mother-in-law had been so serious, so intense and now Lorna was the same.

Her thoughts halted abruptly as she realized with a sudden jolt that she always thought of Lorna as a Rawlinson. Never as belonging to her own family.

Chapter Eight

Instinctively Lorna headed in the direction of the ornamental lake. She couldn't bear to see Doug dismantling Gran's cottage. And she had no time for his silent, anaemic-looking son, Andrew. She wanted to be with Mark and to escape her mother's cheerful high spirits.

She looked at the ruins of the great house as she passed. These days it was gaunt and blackened, gutted in a mysterious blaze one weekend long after the Judds had left. The lower windows were boarded up and the house had stood empty for years. Local children were warned that the building was dangerous.

Lorna wondered – as she so often had – just how the Judds' daughter had died. She had plied her grandmother with questions. A fall, that was all Gran would tell her, that and the fact that the girl never regained consciousness. Then she pursed her lips in a way that meant she would say no more. Lorna had known it was useless to probe.

She felt Mark's presence here in the gardens. Today she was chided by her imaginary brother. "You should be more pleasant to Doug and his son." She knew he was right. He would have had a more generous spirit.

She looked through the tangled, bare February undergrowth for signs of any of the shrubs which Mark had planted. But the month had brought the desolate face of death to the gardens.

She followed the pathway down the moss-covered steps to the oval-shaped lake, hidden from the gaze of the house by huge shrubs. Something was flowering here. With delight Laura pushed the briars to one side and discovered a little bush standing quite erect, its branches covered with pinkish-lavender flowers.

A daphne. She knew that from the drawings she had studied. It was such a pretty name. Lorna handled it lovingly. This was no wild, chance shrub: it had been planted in those days when guests would take the air in a stroll on the terrace by the lake.

Suddenly her eye caught a glimmer of sky-blue nodding in the dense undergrowth. Perhaps something else was in bloom. She pushed her way through the shrubs. They moved slightly with the rustle of the wind – but she could find nothing. It must have been her imagination.

At one end of the lake stood a chipped and battered cherub, now partly covered in creeper. His blank eyes had surveyed all the many changing scenes here. Lorna walked over and leaned against him, lost in her favourite daydream.

She was back in the days of splendour at the great house. How often she had pictured that scene, and drawn herself into it as the gracious lady of the manor showing her guests round the garden, charming them all with her bright, witty conversation.

Sometimes alone at home she would try on her mother's old dance dresses as she acted out the role of the popular hostess.If only it were so easy to be charming in real life. Lorna wondered why it was so much harder to be nice to people in ordinary life.

It was later, when making tracks across the village green, back to the cottage for lunch, that her heart missed a beat. There he was. Tall and handsome with beautiful wavy hair, Christopher Gait was the vicar's son and elder brother of her schoolfriend Anna. She had so often admired at a distance this boy who was cricket captain at his school.

"Coming to our house?" The seventeen-year-old smiled with a mature courtesy.

"No. We're cleaning out Gran's cottage." Lorna was filled with confusion.

"Well, I'm sure we'll see you soon." And he was off.

He had recognized her! To be noticed by Christopher Gait. His words spun round and round in her head as she searched them for any deeper meaning.

She ran her hands through her hair. She could feel bits of twig caught up in it. Her clothes were untidy and soiled from scrambling round the gardens. He would hardly be likely to take any interest in her.

Back at the cottage her mother was looking sunny – and very attractive, Lorna noticed ruefully. Mrs Rawlinson was one of those people who always managed to look immaculate, even in old clothes and in the midst of dirty tasks like clearing out cupboards.

Her mother had gone to a lot of trouble over their lunch. She had spent the previous evening in the kitchen using their precious ration to make a meat loaf. Doug was full of praise.

"I'll just have bread," said Andrew. "I don't like meat loaf." There was a decisiveness rather than rudeness in his voice. Doug glowered.

"Try it. It's quite different to the one you have had. Much nicer. You'll never know if you like things if you won't try anything new."

But Andrew was not to be moved. He fished out a little wallet from his pocket and silently spread out rows of stamps as he munched his bread. They were all of birds, Lorna noticed.

She herself could hardly concentrate on her food, entranced by the thought of Christopher Gait. Her mind sought for excuses to go round to the vicarage.

"What have you been doing with yourself then?" Doug asked Lorna pleasantly.

"Walking." Mrs Rawlinson looked at her uncommunicative daughter with a mixture of puzzlement and annoyance. She opened her mouth as if to speak but snapped it shut again quickly.

"I keep trying to persuade Andrew to take more exercise. He is always either poring over his stamps or sitting with a fishing rod."

There was something slightly scornful about his son's expression as Doug went off to the kitchen to make a cup of tea.

"Barbie!" Lorna's eyebrows shot up at the intimacy of the name. No one had ever called her mother that name in her hearing before.

"I've found a huge bunch of keys. One of them will probably unlock the trinket case."

Chapter Nine

The wind had begun to rise. It was a mournful sound. Lorna heard a metal dustbin lid clatter as it was tossed along the ground by a powerful gust. Mother and daughter drew a little nearer to the fireplace.

Mrs Rawlinson turned on the wireless and began carefully darning her best pair of stockings. The variety programme helped to dispel her irritation with Lorna's churlish behaviour.

She had agreed to keep furniture she didn't want, just because of the girl's insistence. But nothing could please Lorna. She just wrapped herself up in the past. Now she was struggling to find the right key for the trinket box. If only she could put as much enthusiasm into other things . . .

Lorna persevered patiently, trying one key after another, losing her place and starting again. "Got it!" Her voice was triumphant. Barbara Rawlinson turned the volume of the wireless up slightly. She didn't care what was in her mother-in-law's trinket box.

She knew her husband's mother had had little jewellery. Just a few beads and a wedding and engagement ring worn thin over the years.

Now Lorna was fumbling as she tried to fasten her grandmother's cross round her neck. Gran had often worn it and her mother before her. The back was tarnished and the front pattern of enamelled blue and red flowers slightly chipped. But Lorna loved it for all that.

She was emptying beads from the box when she felt the jewellery tray tilt. For a moment she thought she had broken something. Then she realized there was another hidden layer.

She lifted out the tray gingerly. Underneath were an assortment of old letters and cards. A blue envelope, discoloured with the years, bore the name Mark Wolstenholme written boldly across the front.

Rapidly Lorna turned out the contents. A fragment of heavy damask in a singing cornflower blue, a matching snippet of velvet ribbon and a lock of rich brown hair.

Whose hair? Lorna's family all had the same thick, black, strong locks. She delved back into the envelope. There was a letter. She eased it out.

The heading "The Lodge, Sunday" was written in a round, flamboyant writing. Lorna felt uneasy at reading what was clearly a private letter. But it referred to events that had happened long ago. And it might throw some light on the mystery of the missing sovereigns.

"My beloved Mark," it began. "Take great, great care if you come into the gardens. My father is arranging for a fierce Alsation to guard the place. He is still very, very angry and insists I should go abroad

34

on a long holiday. I will hate every minute of it. You know I only want to be with you.

My loving thoughts will be with you every moment. Look after yourself, my darling. You are very precious to me. I'll come just as soon as you send for me.

I want you to take these mementoes of me on your journey. There is something else I want you to have, too. I'll leave it tonight in the spot where you always find me.

All my love—"

Lorna found it hard to decipher the flourishing signature. The only girl's name it resembled was Rosie.

But why hadn't Mark taken the lock of hair and the blue material with him, Lorna wondered. Why should Gran have had the girl's love letter? Perhaps there had been a lovers' quarrel. Maybe it had a connection with Rosie's death. He may never have collected the present she had left for him.

By now Mrs Rawlinson was taking an interest in Lorna's findings, despite herself.

"Did you ever hear what the girl was called?" Lorna inquired. Her mother shook her head. She picked up the blue ribbon thoughtfully. "I do remember someone saying she was known as the girl in blue in the village because she always had a blue ribbon in her hair."

"I suppose Mr Dean might know something," she added helpfully. "He knew your grandmother all her life."

There were other old sentimental letters and cards in the trinket box. Gran had kept hand-drawn

Christmas cards made by Lorna's father as a child. There were sympathy letters written on the deaths of her husband and only son.

Lorna opened one flimsy Christmas card. "Things going well. I hope to have a home by summer. With love to all from Mark. P O Box 42, Rafferty Falls, Alberta, Canada."

"I suppose Gran must have written and told him that Rosie had died," Lorna mused. "She probably warned him to disappear because there was trouble with the police here." That made sense of Gran's fierce instruction that he must not write.

She stared at the address. Mark could be anywhere now. It must be more than forty years since he had sent that card. Nevertheless a crazy idea formed in her mind. Now she had an address she would write to Mark and tell him of Gran's death. There was just a million-to-one chance that the letter would find him.

Lorna felt a thrill of secret pleasure at her plan. She resolved to tell nobody. After all, other people would probably only laugh.

Chapter Ten

Lorna plied old Mr Dean with questions. He was helpful but vague.

"They never did find the money that I ever heard," he commented. "But I never did trust the Judds. He were a ruthless, selfish man and his wife were a poor thing, did as she were told. But the girl, now she were a right pretty lass. Always in blue she was. Miss Lavender Blue we called her."

Lorna pictured Miss Lavender Blue dancing round the ornamental lake.

"It were a wild, wet night when she fell in the gardens," he recalled. "No one could think why she were out on a night like that. She were still breathing when they found here. But she never did come round."

"Do you think she had gone to meet Mark?"

"I wouldn't know," he replied slowly. "But that is what old Mr Judd thought."

"Would anyone else in the village remember Mark?"

The old man thought hard. "Not as I can recall. Most of them are long since gone. Emily were one of the last."

Lorna hugged herself with delight at the thought of her secret letter to Mark. She had written everything down, bought the special stamp for Canada and posted it off.

She decided it was time to take Patch for a walk, intent as she was on rediscovering Mark's plants in the grounds of the big house.

She had stared so often at Mark's drawings that she had committed many of the plants and leaves to memory. Now as the days were beginning to lengthen and the early buds to appear she had one or two successes.

What a joy it had been to spot the silvery-green catkins of the *Garrya elliptica* so early in the year. She knew that Mark had planted this now huge shrub. She had gathered some of the branches and taken them home.

Lorna came to the village more and more often these days. It wasn't just a question of taking Patch for walks.

Most weeks she had tea at the vicarage after school on Fridays. She and Anna had both been chosen to take part in the school play, "Little Women", a dramatized version of the famous book. Predictably Anna was the heroine, Jo, Lorna her sharp-tongued sister, Amy. Together they would rehearse their lines.

Lorna always hoped she would have a chance to talk to Christopher. But if he was in the house, he never appeared while the girls were there.

Lorna revelled in the vicarage atmosphere, the huge, rambling old kitchen, the homeliness of Mrs

Gait with her thick woollen clothes and plait of long hair twisted round her head.

She envied Anna the security of it all. No coming home to light a fire in the damp front room. No waiting to hear the factory whistle which meant her mother would be returning. No Doug . . . She could not imagine his brash self-confidence and wireless catch phrases fitting into this world.

There was a solidity about the Gaits' way of life which she longed for. The vicar's "reading teas", when he would prop a book up while he ate his food, were just the sort of world her father would have relished. More and more she herself felt drawn to this world, away from the dinginess of Princess Street.

One afternoon Lorna sat alone in the vicarage sitting room, learning her lines, half hearing the piano music which was drifting into the room. She felt herself standing once more by her father's side on the moorland. It was a bright, autumn day, the wind sweeping the sharp grass to and fro in a gentle, tidal movement. Patch was off chasing a stick her father had thrown.

She felt her father's face very close to her, his eyes looking at her with tender concern. He said nothing but took his daughter's hand firmly as they walked through the springy turf. It was the sort of day when the silvery line of the sea shone on the horizon.

It was a small, real scene which had remained imprinted on Lorna's memory. In a strange way she had known at the time that this was a moment she would never forget and she had accordingly etched every detail in her mind.

Tears were rolling down her cheeks when she became aware that Anna had returned into the room and was looking at her. She felt embarrassed and foolish.

"It's the music." Anna's voice was kind and gentle. "It's Rachmaninov's piano concerto, the second one, and it is terribly sad."

The chords of the piano had unlocked Lorna's deep sense of loss, her longing for her dead father . . . At the time of his death she had cried very little. She had not been able to comprehend that she would never see him again.

At that moment Lorna resolved that she must learn to play the piano. The music was a way of reaching out to her father. It would create a magic bond between them.

Chapter Eleven

Barbara Rawlinson turned the key in the door. It had been a lovely evening. She was humming softly as she entered 102, Princess Street, followed closely by Doug.

They were not late. It was the first time that Lorna had offered to stay in on her own and Mrs Rawlinson had insisted on getting home promptly to make sure her daughter was all right.

Her heel caught on a piece of paper. Not those old sketches again, she thought crossly. Lorna barely looked up as they entered. Old yellowed and dusty drawings were laid out all over the living room floor.

"Don't stand on them," she demanded unreasonably but that was asking the impossible.

Within seconds her mother's sunny spirits had evaporated. She had come home eager to see that all was well with Lorna. Now she wished she had stayed at the dance a little longer.

She stepped gingerly over the drawings, pausing to take off her coat.

"I'll take that, love," offered Doug eagerly, stepping forward. He helped her out of her coat and as he did so he leaned forward and put his arm round her shoulder affectionately.

At that moment Lorna looked up sharply. She saw the gesture and a look of pain shot across her face.

There was a slight gasp and she rushed across the room, trampling regardless on the precious drawings. Upstairs they heard her bedroom door slam shut behind her.

For Mrs Rawlinson the evening was ruined. She could hear sobs from Lorna's bedroom and began silently to pick up the pictures.

She switched on the wireless. Her whole body echoed the pain she knew her daughter was experiencing. But there was anger too. Why couldn't she enjoy Doug's company? What was so wrong about it?

She had spent night after night making Lorna a costume for the school play, unpicking old garments to adapt them into something suitable. Why couldn't she now have some fun?

With heavy deliberation she went into the kitchen and put on the kettle. She would make a cup of tea for Doug. Lorna would just have to grow up and realize that she too had a life to lead. She had felt carefree and happy that evening – until she got home.

"I don't know what is eating her," commented Doug as he sipped his tea. Mrs Rawlinson didn't comment. She understood all too well what was upsetting Lorna.

She recalled Lorna's unguarded expression when she saw the large card her mother had received on

St Valentine's Day. It had been Lorna who had dived for the post. But there was only one card.

It was after Doug had left that she climbed the stairs to Lorna's room. She opened the door slowly. Her daughter lay face down with her head in the pillow, her body racked with sobs.

"Will you tell me what is wrong?" Mrs Rawlinson's voice had a sharpness to it.

Lorna did not move. Her mother put her hands on her shoulders.

"Lorna, sit up! You are being unfair to me. Stop this carry-on."

Her daughter sat up, her face distorted with weeping.

"Now we have got to have this out," said her mother firmly.

"I just spoil your fun." Lorna's voice was bitter. "I get in the way. You should have seen your face when I said I would stay in on my own."

"What do you want me to do, Lorna? Stay at home for the rest of my life? I've been in nearly every night for the last four years trying to look after us both."

Barbara Rawlinson felt her voice beginning to rise. "Do you ever think what life is like for me?" she demanded. Her fingers shook as she lit a cigarette.

Lorna stared back, miserable and unrepentant.

"You have never bothered to try to be polite to Doug." Her mother's voice was accusing. "What have you got against him?"

"He's not good enough for you," Lorna replied bluntly. "He's so smarmy and . . ." Her voice trailed away. She had been about to say "vulgar".

Her mother had become much calmer. "Do you mean he is not good enough for me? Or is he not good

43

enough for you?" The question struck home.

"He is nothing like my father."

"No. He's not, I know that, Lorna. But maybe that is a good thing. You can't just replace people with someone the same."

Mrs Rawlinson paused. "I know how much you loved your father. I did too, Lorna. But it is four years since he died. We all have to go on living. Nobody is perfect. I know what you think about Doug. You make it obvious. He is just an ordinary fellow. But Lorna, you must realize your father wasn't perfect. There were times when he was very difficult. And stubborn. Life wasn't easy for me."

Barbara Rawlinson's mind went back to some of the times when her husband had withdrawn into his private world, cut off from her: she had felt acutely lonely and miserable.

She stroked Lorna's hair. The misery on the girl's face tugged at her inside.

"I know." Lorna struggled to find the right words. "I should be nicer to Doug, I know. But it hurts so much to see him sitting in Dad's place. He doesn't fit."

Mrs Rawlinson put her arm round her daughter's shoulder and hugged her. Lorna had had a bad year, losing Gran, not being able to keep Patch. She spent far too much time on her own. If only she would go out and enjoy herself.

If somehow she could get a piano . . . Lorna kept asking for one but her mother could think of no way she could afford either the instrument or the lessons. If only there were some way . . . It might be a new interest, something to give her pleasure.

Mrs Rawlinson's arms were wrapped around her daughter reassuringly as Lorna's body was convulsed with sobs, partly from sorrow but more from shame.

Chapter Twelve

The school play had been a great success. Lorna glowed with the praise she had received. She had felt in her element. Her mother had been so proud. She had come alone to the performance: Lorna had been relieved about that.

Now that the applause and compliments had died down, she was left with a sense of anti-climax. For other people mounting anticipation began to grip the air. The war was drawing to a close. Girls in her class were demonstrating a mixture of excitement and apprehension at the return of fathers they had not seen for years.

But for Lorna the coming of spring with all its optimism brought little joy. Talk of fathers returning did nothing to help.

Doug was trying hard to please her. When Lorna arrived home with some plants she had dug up from the garden of the big house, in no time at all he had found an old sink which he filled with soil to give her a small garden in the backyard.

He had brought a few cuttings from his own home. Lorna hadn't the heart to say she didn't want them, that she was collecting Mark's shrubs.

Now the play was over she had less opportunity to go to the vicarage. Every now and then she caught sight of the tall, striking figure of Christopher Gait and each time felt herself flush. He was so handsome, so unattainable. What hope had a girl like her, awkward and plain, of being noticed by such an Adonis?

She willed the clouds scurrying across the sky to make him fall for her. She whispered his name to the night sky. She would daydream of rescuing him from a burning house or gently nursing him back to health after a dangerous illness.

But no amount of will or magic seemed to entice him. He remained far out of reach. If they met he always acknowledged her pleasantly. But no more than that.

With Doug's son Andrew there was altogether too much solid reality. No more enthusiastic about the arrangement than Lorna, the pale, thin boy often found himself taking his weekend meals at Princess Street.

He ate very little and could not be persuaded to try anything he did not want. Mrs Rawlinson was always coaxing. "Just try a little," she would say. "I put good things in it. It will build you up."

But Andrew did not budge. He seldom offered open opposition to anything: he simply did not join in. When his father prevailed upon him to play Monopoly, a game Lorna loved and always won, he went through the motions without making any attempt to win.

47

"Don't you want Vine Street?" demanded Lorna, holding the property that would have given him a set.

"Don't mind," he replied flatly. "It isn't going to make any difference, is it? You are going to win." Lorna's enthusiasm for the game immediately vanished.

It was hard to know what would bring Andrew to life – unless it was a book of jokes. Then occasionally he would curl up in an armchair and laugh away to himself.

Lorna resented the frequent presence of Doug and Andrew in her home. She liked to spread her books around the living room and to be left to her own devices. Now her mother was endlessly tidying up and worrying how things looked.

She had no time for Andew or anything he was interested in – fishing, stamps or joke books. Mark would have chased across the moors with a dog. To sit by a reservoir with a fishing line for hours on end, never!

Sometimes the two would walk to the reservoir together, Andrew with his fishing line, Lorna on her way to the village to take out Patch.

She would go, on these occasions, with strangely mixed-up feelings. Part of her longed to be free of Princess Street and away from Doug. Another part twisted inwardly at the thought of leaving him alone with her mother.

She and Andrew would exchange only the most minimal comments. Lorna was too busy daydreaming of her imaginary brother. There had been no answer from the real Mark at Rafferty Falls. Not that she was surprised. The chance of her letter reaching him had been as slight as if she had put a message in a bottle and thrown it out to sea.

"What do you do up there?" inquired Andrew one afternoon, breaking in on her reverie. "Don't you get bored wandering around with that dog?"

Lorna was taken aback. She knew what it was like to be lonely. And to be unhappy. But bored? No.

"Actually," she announced, "I'm looking for special plants round the lake. My great uncle planted them. He was the estate manager at the big house in the old days."

She could have bitten off her tongue as soon as she had spoken: Andrew might have heard of the disgrace. But the boy registered no sign of this. Instead his face lit up.

"I know there are some very unusual plants," he ventured. "Some of them are foreign. I recognized them from my stamps. They must have been terribly rich, the family who lived up there. My grandmother used to help in the kitchens. They had great banquets. She goes on about all the fancy food they made."

Andrew's grandmother at the big house! She must have known the daughter of the family. She would be able to recall Mark. Lorna was riveted. What did she know of the scandal?

"Does she talk about the family at the great house?" she asked.

"Mmn. But it's all jumbled up. My nan chatters all the time. I don't listen to most of it."

"Do you think I could talk to her?" Lorna was eager. "I want to find out more about my great uncle."

"Should think so."

"Next weekend?"

"No." Andrew's voice was surprisingly decisive. "I've got to go away next weekend."

"Where?"

"Away."

"I gathered that, silly. But where?"

"My mother's." Lorna couldn't fail to notice the twisted expression that came over his face.

"What is so bad about that?" she inquired brusquely.

"Him. I hate him." The answer was spat out ferociously.

With a flash of illumination Lorna understood how he felt. That was how she responded to Doug. She wondered, for the first time, if Andrew resented her mother. She did not ask – in case he did. She could feel hostile towards her mother but she could not bear criticism of her from anyone else. She had hated it whenever a momentary look of disapproval had shot across Gran's face.

It was only when she was up on the moors alone, tossing a stick to Patch, her eyes following the kestrels as they swooped low over the grassland, that it occurred to her that she was luckier than Andrew.

He might have two parents but at least she knew that her picture of her father would never change. She would never lose his love and admiration. Nobody could take away from her the pride she felt in him, or the knowlege that he believed in her. For the first time she felt a wave of sympathy for Andrew. He so clearly hated the thought of visiting his mother and her new husband.

There was nothing at which Andrew particularly shone. He wasn't sporty or clever or specially good-looking. Really, thought Lorna, feeling an unexpected warmth towards him, he has not got a lot going for him.

Chapter Thirteen

Lorna mentioned the idea of visiting Andrew's grandmother once or twice but the moment never seemed to be opportune. Yes, it would be fine, said Doug, but so far he hadn't come up with a suggested time.

Up at the big house Lorna's eager examining eyes spotted buds appearing as spring stirred the gardens back into life. With the help of Mark's drawings and a gardening encyclopaedia she pressed on with her detective work. She began to suspect that the flower-beds around the lake were arranged in particular colour patterns, all yellow, white or blue. But it was too early in the year to be sure.

At school she was working frantically hard. Exams loomed ahead and she was determined to do well. She might never be chosen to be the form monitor or prefect but when it came to schoolwork Lorna knew she was as good as the others.

More and more she was conscious of a distance

between herself and the other girls. Their mothers were waiting in comfortable homes when they got back from school. They had real brothers and sisters. Her problems were not theirs, their lives so different.

Anna was a good and loyal friend but her world was so far removed from Princess Street that Lorna hesitated to invite her home.

She was too proud to confide her innermost feelings to anyone, the hostility she still felt towards Doug, her dismissal of Andrew, the pain which recurred whenever she thought of her father and Gran.

There was no one with whom to share her memories, except her mother. And when, very rarely, they did talk about the past, it seemed as if they were remembering different events, so opposed were their recollections.

Only the imaginary Mark could share her private world.

At the vicarage Anna and her family were involved in organizing a dance in the village hall. With the new lightness of spirit at large everybody seemed to be going.

Lorna hesitated briefly when Anna tried to sell her a ticket. Christopher would be sure to be there. But no. It was no good. In any case she had nothing to wear. In breaktimes girls at school would be practising dance steps while she buried herself in a book.

It was her mother who announced that Doug had bought tickets for them all, Andrew and Lorna included.

"I can't go. I have far too much work to do. There are exams in a few weeks."

"What nonsense, Lorna. You never stop working. It's a Saturday night – for goodness sake, have a bit of fun. You can't work every night. And there is Andrew. He'll be glad of your company."

Eventually Lorna relented. Yes, she would go.

Chapter Fourteen

Barbara Rawlinson was so looking forward to the village dance, she longed to envelop her daughter in her own enthusiasm.

She looked at Lorna anxiously. It was not just that the girl was squarely built: she seemed almost wilfully determined to make herself graceless and heavy.

A chrysalis, thought Mrs Rawlinson, reassuring herself that this was just a difficult stage from which something assured and fully-formed would eventually break out.

That gave birth to a new idea. There was an old silk dress of her mother-in-law's which she had kept. The style was quite out of date but the fabric was good. She had thought of using it to make something for herself. But no. This would be better.

Night after night in the dim light of the gas mantles she sat patiently unpicking all the seams with nail scissors. She didn't want to waste a scrap of the precious fabric.

Lorna would shine in it. She would be the butterfly at the ball. From this rich blue fabric the mother was determined to create her daughter's first dance dress. No longer would she secretly have to try on her mother's old gowns. She would have one of her own.

It was slow and demanding work, particularly as she could not fit the half-made gown on Lorna. She was determined that this would be a surprise.

As it was, Lorna was so absorbed in her schoolwork and her own activities that she never inquired what her mother was making. Just what she herself was going to wear, Mrs Rawlinson had no idea. That didn't concern her. She wanted this to be Lorna's evening.

"Lorna," her mother called out one evening as she finished the ironing. "Can you come over here?"

"What for?" Reluctantly Lorna broke off from her biology homework and walked over to her mother who stood holding the long dress.

Mrs Rawlinson's eyes were sparkling with delight. "I've made this for you. Come, try it on. I do want to see how you look in it."

Lorna was appalled when she looked at the dress. So this was what her mother had been busy with, night after night! It was exquisite and immaculately made – but for someone else. All frills and flounces, it was not her sort of dress at all. She couldn't wear it. She would be the laughing stock of the girls at school.

She caught the anxious look in her mother's eyes and tried hard to smile.

"It's lovely," she managed with a false brightness in her voice, conscious of how much loving care had gone into its making. "I'll go and put it on."

"I do hope it fits all right. I had to guess the waist. Don't crush it!"

The dress required only the slightest adjustments to fit perfectly. The workmanship was superb. But Lorna surveyed herself in the mirror with horror. The off-the-shoulder style, the silky drapes across her strong arms, looked dreadfully wrong.

Fortunately her mother seemed unaware of her dismay. "I've got enough coupons to get you some new shoes. And you will need something round your neck." Mrs Rawlinson chattered on. "There might be something in Gran's box which would be suitable."

"The dress is beautiful, Mum. Thank you." Lorna kissed her mother lightly on the cheek and managed to escape to her own room before the tears streamed down her cheeks. Guilt and gratitude mingled indissolubly.

She turned her attention to Gran's trinket box, looking for a necklace. Suddenly it occurred to her that this dress material was very like the snippet of blue fabric which had lain in the box for years. She fingered it.

What, she wondered, would Rosie's dress have been like? Elegant and classical, she imagined. But then Rosie would not have looked like her.

Chapter Fifteen

Lorna stood ill at ease in her blue frilly dress ready for the dance, complete with silver open-toed sandals on which her mother had lavished her last clothing coupons.

Even Barbara Rawlinson acknowledged that something was wrong. "It's your hair," she said, holding it back. "I know, we will turn the ends under."

She lit a ring on their gas cooker and put in a pair of curling tongs to heat. Never before had they tried to curl Lorna's hair.

She sat on a chair while her mother worked away with the tongs. "I'll just brush it into shape," her mother said at last and she went off to fetch a hairbrush.

Lorna stood up and faced herself in the mirror. She was aghast. There was a thick frizz all over the ends of her wiry dark hair. She looked like a tawdry fairy on top of the Christmas tree! Returning with the hairbrush, her mother saw the tears of humiliation fill her eyes.

She was just trying to comb some water through the frizz when the doorbell rang. Doug stood there with Andrew. His hair shone almost as much as his black patent leather shoes and he was sporting a particularly bold tie for the occasion.

Andrew hovered in the background. When he saw Lorna in all her finery, his face broke momentarily into a half-smile.

Lorna wanted the ground to swallow her up. She kept trying to smooth down her hair with her hands. Andrew looked equally uncomfortable in his new clothes. For once Lorna was glad of his presence: there was someone else to share her discomfort.

A lively hubbub filled the village hall as Lorna and her family entered. She noticed how Doug grasped her mother's arm possessively. Mrs Rawlinson looked delicate and pretty, as always, and clearly he was proud to be escorting her. Quickly they were surrounded by friends from work who came up to them, laughing and chatting.

Lorna caught sight of Anna in the distance. Her friend was wearing a simple green summer dress, her long, blonde hair falling loosely about her shoulders. Lorna remained firmly positioned by her mother's side. She didn't want her schoolfriends to see her like this.

"What a lovely dress!" Lorna found her gown was being admired by one of her mother's work friends. "This your daughter, then? She must take after her dad."

Barbara Rawlinson nodded. Doug returned with a round of drinks. There was lemonade for Lorna and Andrew. But where was Andrew?

She peered round the hall but could see no sign of him.

"He'll have found some friends, I don't doubt." Doug didn't sound concerned.

Lorna's mother regarded her anxiously. "Do you want to go over to your schoolfriends?"

Lorna shook her head. That was the last thing she wanted. The only place she wanted to be was as far away from here as possible. She drank her lemonade with grim determination.

"Come on!" Put that glass down and have this dance with me!" Doug steered the reluctant Lorna on to the floor. It was packed. Stiff and self-conscious, she didn't know what to do. But Doug held her firmly and led her into the steps.

It wasn't difficult. This was a Valetta and Lorna found herself able to copy the couple ahead. Soon she was drawn into the spontaneous gaiety of the dance, laughing happily.

Her heart missed a beat when she caught sight of Christopher Gait across the room. He was dancing with a dark-haired girl she recognized as one of the sixth formers at school.

The band played loudly and enthusiastically. People demanded an encore and by the time the dance finally drew to a close, Lorna was panting and slightly dishevelled, her face shining with enjoyment.

A couple of husbands of her mother's friends asked her to dance before Anna spotted Lorna and dragged her over to the group of young people.

"You look very grand," commented Anna tactfully. "Your dress is a lovely colour." Lorna was the only one in a long dress.

Anna and their schoolfriends stood together, giggling and commenting on the antics of those on the floor. There were few unattached boys available and those there were seemed reluctant to dance. They stood propping up the walls of the village hall.

Immediately before every dance there was an expectant hush among the group of schoolgirls. Whenever a young man advanced in their direction, Lorna experienced a wave of nervous expectation which subsided in disappointment as he approached someone else.

Anna squealed slightly when a tall, spotty boy stammered out his request before leading her self-consciously on to the floor. Once a dance was in progress some girls danced together in pairs. Others talked to one another with forced animation to show everyone what a good time they were having.

Christopher Gait nodded in Lorna's direction. He won many admiring glances as he moved about the hall, looking particularly distinguished in his cricket team blazer. But whenever he danced it was with the same dark-haired girl.

She must be in heaven, Lorna thought, experiencing the gnawing pains of envy, surprised as she was at Christopher's choice. Tall and strong-featured, his girlfriend was not conventionally pretty. But Lorna knew her to be clever, with a place waiting for her at Cambridge.

Familiar faces swirled around the floor. Every now and then she caught sight of her mother, dancing sometimes with Doug, sometimes with other men in the group.

Anna returned to Lorna's side. "I hope he doesn't ask me again." But her eyes glowed nevertheless with delight at the compliment of being asked.

No one invited Lorna to dance and her expression was frozen into a nonchalant mask when another teenager led Anna back on to the floor, leaving her standing conspicuously alone. She wondered where

Andrew was. She had not seen him all evening.

In many hours wandering by herself on the hillside, Lorna had never felt so much alone as here in this crowded hall. Even the imaginary Mark could provide little support here. Pride demanded a real flesh-and-blood partner.

Lorna vowed never to do this again. It was like being put up for auction and finding nobody wanted to buy. She moved to a chair and sat down.

The music was romantic and nostalgic. A local singer began to croon a love song. Lights in the dance hall were dimmed as couples moved slowly round the floor, holding one another tightly. Anna hadn't returned from the previous dance.

Lorna stared at the scene like a visitor peering through a window at a gathering to which she has not been invited. She was grateful for the subdued lighting.

She caught sight of her mother and Doug on the dance floor. They were very close, her mother's head resting on Doug's shoulder. He was looking down at her adoringly, with clearly not a thought for anyone else.

The same blind, unreasoning indignation and distress that Lorna had experienced once before in Princess Street took possession of her again and a stab of physical pain that was a mixture of jealousy and revulsion made her rush out of the nearest door.

Chapter Sixteen

Lorna stepped from a scene of noisy animation to the hush of a deserted village. The cool night air embraced her, almost soothingly. It was a clear starlit night, the moon casting a silvery glow over the scene and lending familiar shapes a sinister mystery.

Some stifled giggles by the village hall made Lorna walk quickly away. Slowly she crossed the village green, noticing sadly a light in a bedroom window of Gran's cottage, now someone else's home.

The village church raised its spire proudly towards a myriad of stars. Lorna shuddered slightly at the eerie shapes cast by the moonlight over the graveyard.

She had no plan in her mind of what she would do. She wrapped her arms around herself in the chill night air, determined not to return to the dance hall, rebellious yet half hoping it would not be long before her mother noticed she was missing and set out to find her.

Lorna glanced across the valley. This light lent

even Gauntsford a strange enchantment: the mock castle assumed a real grandeur, offset by the silver sheen of the reservoir.

She shuddered again. The humiliation of the dance hall scene was still raw and she felt a physical longing for her father, for Gran, for Mark . . . for someone to care for and understand her.

Instinctively her feet followed their familiar path down towards the big house and the ornamental lake. Long dark shadows played around her but Lorna's natural apprehension was drowned by a strange wave of indifference.

She no longer cared what happened to her. She even acknowledged a twisted satisfaction at the thought of her mother's sense of guilt and what she would suffer if a disaster befell Lorna.

As she made her way steadily and purposefully towards the lake she could just hear in the distance the rhythmic vibrations of the dance band in the village hall. Her dress caught on a shrub. She pulled it free, tugging angrily, and heard the sound of material tear – without remorse. She hated the dress.

The ruins of the big house looked ugly and forbidding. Darkly menacing, it spoke only of vanity and ambition. It wasn't a house in which anybody could have been happy. The light of the cold, dead moon lent it a chilling, ghostly mystery.

Lorna felt that someone was gazing at her. Looking up at one of the windows she saw what could have been a face staring down from among the shadowy reflections. She thought she saw it move.

She shivered, suddenly afraid. It might be hours before she was missed.

There was a movement in the undergrowth. Some twigs snapped and she felt as if her heart jumped into her mouth. It must be the breeze whistling from across the moors, she assured herself forcibly.

But the night was still. The leaves weren't moving anywhere else. She quickened her pace towards the lake. With a mounting sense of horror she realized that she hadn't imagined the noise: something was moving through the shrubs, coming steadily towards her. Closer and closer.

Her pursuer was gaining ground. The rustling of leaves behind her was like the rustling of a silk dress. Lorna began to run, but her ball gown kept catching on the briars. She arrived at the top of the steps that led down to the lake.

A pain gripped her chest and something caught in her throat as she stood there, breathless and terrified.

Then she saw her by the cherub, her strained, white face looking up at Lorna beseechingly: a beautiful young woman in a blue dress that had a steely shine in the moonlight. She was moving steadily towards Lorna.

She seemed to glide along the lakeside, her arms held out all the while in a welcoming gesture. Lorna's fear evaporated and she stepped forward as if possessed.

In a flash she saw the smile of the girl's face turn to a look of horror. Her hands went out as if to push Lorna back just as she put a foot forward to descend the steps. It skidded over a patch of moss and Lorna lost her balance. She threw out her arms but there was nothing to grab to steady herself. She felt herself falling down, down, down.

For a second she seemed to be floating. Then came the crashing blow as her head hit the paving stones. Fleetingly she wondered how much she'd hurt herself, just how painful it would be when she came to.

Surprisingly she felt no hurt, just a warm comfortable feeling sweeping over her as she drifted from consciousness, aware that she was leaving all the pain behind. She was moving effortlessly into a garden full of flowers and the young woman, now happily smiling, was advancing towards her. As she did so she ran her hand through long blue catkins with slender grey-green fingers.

Chapter Seventeen

Lorna stretched out her arms and felt the soft comfort of the sheets. Very gradually and reluctantly she opened her eyes, uncertain of what was to greet her.

She was in a strange room, surrounded by unfamiliar heavy furniture. The thick dark curtains let in so little light, that it was impossible to judge the time of day. In panic she shot up in bed. Where was she? The sudden jolt made everything spin round alarmingly and, feeling sick, she sank back into the pillow in confusion.

"Lorna!" The creaking of the bed had brought her mother rushing to her side. Her voice was high with anxiety and emotion.

"What's happened?" Lorna's voice emerged as a hoarse croak. It was an effort to speak. She felt exhausted.

Her mother laid her hand gently on her forehead. "You fell down the steps by the lake but you're safe and well here in the vicarage. You are going to be all right but you must stay in bed for a few days." Gently she raised Lorna's head with her hands and kissed her cheek.

Weak as she was, Lorna was conscious of the happiness and relief in her mother's choking voice. Her head throbbed mercilessly as she tried to lift it and the room spun round.

"Don't move!" Her mother's voice was emphatic.

"Mrs Gait! Lorna has come round." Two heads were bearing down on her, talking in whispers.

Lorna closed her eyes again. She must get back to her dream. It was important. She had something to do.

"Lorna! Lorna! Open your eyes again." It was her mother's agitated plea that forced her to drag herself back to the everyday world.

"Try and stay awake a little while." This time it was Mrs Gait's voice. "You've been asleep so long."

Lorna struggled to do as she was told. Mrs Gait went off to fetch the village doctor. Her mother refused to move from her side, stroking her hand constantly.

For a time Lorna seemed to float backwards and forwards. She had to find the plant with the long, blue catkins. It was vital that she should dig it up.

"I've got to go down to the gardens." She sat up in bed violently.

"You'll do no such thing. You've got to stay exactly where you are for a few days." The doctor's manner allowed no argument. "You've twisted your ankle badly and you've got some nasty bruises. I'm afraid you will have quite a lot of aches and pains for a while but you are a very lucky girl indeed to be alive."

He managed to sound both friendly and admonishing at the same time.

He was giving directions in a low, authoritative voice to the two women. "You should bathe her bottom lip in a salt solution. She bit it badly when she fell and it will be highly sensitive for a time."

Lorna could remember nothing of the fall and she felt too weak to take any interest in what was happening. Every time she shifted her position some bit of her made a painful protest.

Chapter Eighteen

Mrs Rawlinson had to return to Princess Street and to work as soon as the doctor allowed Lorna downstairs a few days later. It was decided that the patient should stay on at the vicarage to recuperate. There she would have company during the day – and someone to keep an eye on her.

Little by little recollections of the nightmarish evening and of the fall came back to Lorna. And with them came an overwhelming sense of shame. "You fool," she told herself for the hundredth time, clenching her fists, when she was on her own. At night she would bury her head in her pillow to try to escape the waves of embarrassment which would sweep over her. She was grateful that the Gaits avoided the subject completely.

"Who found me?" inquired Lorna as she and her mother were sitting alone by the vicarage fire. Each evening Mrs Rawlinson would walk up to the village straight after work to see how her daughter was progressing.

"Andrew. He had abandoned the dance – like you. He had planned it all in advance and hidden his fishing tackle by the lake. He was sitting there alone when he saw you suddenly appear and crash down the steps. The poor lad was in a real state of shock when he got back to the hall. He thought you were dead."

Mrs Rawlinson shuddered visibly at the thought of what might have been.

"Did he see the girl in blue?" Lorna asked quickly.

Her mother looked blank.

"There was no one else there."

"She was there," Lorna insisted. "She followed me from the big house. Surely Andrew must have seen her beckoning me?"

Mrs Rawlinson looked worried. Was Lorna delirious?

"There was someone behind me all the time in the bushes," Lorna persisted.

Her mother looked puzzled for a few moments. Then her face lightened.

"Of course. It was Patch," she said with sudden inspiration. "Mr Dean had let him out into the garden before he locked up for the night. He couldn't understand why the dog didn't come back when he called. He was sitting guarding you when we came back with Andrew."

Was it really just the friendly Patch who had been pursuing her? Had it all been just a dream? Lorna found she could not think straight and sank back into the pillows.

She heard her mother's voice recounting how Doug had carried her back to the vicarage. Lorna winced slightly at the name. It had been a traumatic night for them all. Mrs Rawlinson and Mrs Gait had sat by her bedside waiting for any sign of a return to consciousness. The doctor had been summoned. He had said that all they could do was to wait – and hope.

It had been nearly twenty-four hours before Lorna had re-opened her eyes.

Mrs Rawlinson never asked why Lorna had been wandering around the gardens in the middle of the night. No doubt she understood. But Lorna experienced a profound sense of guilt when she saw the unmistakeable signs of strain on her mother's face. She looked worn and tired – and much older than the happy woman who had set out so optimistically to go to the village dance.

Lorna felt a pang of sharp distress, too, when she caught sight of the torn, blood-spattered dress on which her mother had lavished so much loving care.

The days dragged at the vicarage. To her surprise Lorna found herself longing to get back home. But her mother was firm. She must remain where she was until she was stronger.

The Gaits were kind but so busy. Visitors and parishioners were always coming and going. Doors in the house were never shut and Lorna shivered in the large, draughty rooms. There never seemed to be time for them to sit together and talk as a family. Meals were functional rather than companionable. Always there were interruptions.

It was, Lorna decided, rather like living in a railway station. So much through traffic. She longed for the cosy privacy of her own home.

As for Christopher Gait, he treated Lorna with the rather patronizing nonchalance he adopted towards his younger sister. His mind was always on his own activities and Lorna could not fail to notice how often he combed his hair and pressed the waves into place. That did not fit the image of her hero.

With two black eyes, many bruises and cuts as well as swollen cut lips she was freed from any illusion that she might win his romantic attention. Handsome and dashing Christopher undoubtedly was but at close quarters Lorna could no longer view him with the same worshipping eyes. He was no Mark.

Unusually for the Gaits, they all found themselves sitting round the table at lunch one day. The vicar's wife, looking tired, said she had a migraine coming on.

"Will you cycle into Gauntsford to get a prescription for Mrs Ellis?" she asked her son. "There is no way she can get out with the children because the baby is ill. She never asks favours so I offered to get it for her – but I think I am going to have to lie down. My head is beginning to split."

"Mmn." Christopher assented but without any grace. He had several things he must do first. It was nearly closing time when he finally left the house to set out on his errand – only to discover that his bicycle had a flat tyre. Mrs Gait collected the prescription the following morning.

Chapter Nineteen

Lorna was sitting alone one afternoon when she had an unexpected visitor. Old Mr Dean arrived clutching a large bar of chocolate which must have cost him many precious ration coupons.

The old man was nervous and awkward. He had hardly ever set foot in the vicarage and clearly felt ill at ease in what he saw as a rather grand house occupied by his "betters".

He perched on the edge of an armchair. "It is a miracle to see you sitting there so perky," he commented. "Gave me a terrible turn that did. That were some night. I were out on the Green calling Patch when they carried you back. It were like history repeating itself," he mumbled. "Even wearing a blue dress too."

Lorna was weary and her lips hurt sharply when she bit into the chocolate. "What history?" she inquired without much interest.

"The Judds' daughter. 'Twere the same steps. And

a ball too that night." The old man shook his head. "They sat with her too."

Lorna was instantly alert. So Rosie had fallen on those same steps. She shuddered at the thought of how near she had come to the same fate.

"You should never have done that to your poor mother," chided Mr Dean. "The poor woman has had quite enough to put up with – losing her husband like she did."

Lorna changed the subject. "What was Rosie doing on those steps?"

"Rosie? I don't recall as her name was Rosie," the old man puckered his brow. "Doesn't sound right to me, but then my memory lets me down these days. No, no one could ever say why she were out that night. It were wild. There'd been a thunderstorm like you thought it was a punishment on the world.

"She were wearing a long, blue dress, just like you," the old man rambled on. "Whatever made you do a thing like that?" He turned on Lorna sharply, accusingly.

"Emily's only grandchild," his voice trailed away, ignoring the fact that she hadn't answered his question. "Funny thing, there was soil on her hands when they found her. They said she must have been digging. But no one in their right mind would dig on a night like that."

"Digging." The word was the key which unlocked Lorna's memory. She was back in the garden, surrounded by the images she had lived through time and again as she lay feverish in the vicarage bed.

The girl in blue who had beckoned her on was now tugging her by the arm through a maze of plants to a low-growing bush with a shower of tiny catkin-like flowers.

"Dig! Dig!" The girl's voice was urgent, desperate. Lorna stood motionless, uncomprehending, as the girl, with fierce, nervous energy, began to scratch the ground with her delicate fingers. As Lorna bent down towards her she heard the words "Find it, please! Don't stop" and then the figure simply melted away.

"Lorna!" Mrs Gait was shaking her shoulders gently. The old man had rushed to fetch her when the girl relapsed into what he thought was a faint.

Lorna said nothing. She put her hands round the hot drink the vicar's wife pressed upon her. Now she understood.

She knew now, without any doubt, that the girl in blue had led her back in time to the days when the Judds ruled the valley and when the young lady of the household had had the effrontery to fall in love with a humble gardener.

Chapter Twenty

102 Princess Street had never seemed so welcoming. Lorna's mother was standing at the door when she arrived home one Saturday morning, given a lift in the Pikeleigh village store delivery van.

It was only when she stepped out into the open air that Lorna realized how weak she felt – her knees nearly gave way under her – and she gratefully allowed her mother to steer her to a chair in front of a blazing fire.

Her eyes travelled round the room affectionately. "No! Where did you get that?" She was on her feet in an instant, amazement quickly followed by delight. A black upright piano stood against one wall.

"The Millers' Arms were changing their piano and wanted to get rid of the old one. It's not a good one, I'm afraid, and it does need tuning. But it will do for you to learn on." Mrs Rawlinson's voice was apologetic.

Lorna tried out the few scales Anna had taught her.

She ran her hands over the dark wood of the piano, the marks on the front panels where once there had been candelabra. It was stained and chipped in places but wonderful for all that. And hers. That was best of all.

Barbara Rawlinson looked on happily, gratified by Lorna's evident delight.

"It will be a little while before I can afford to pay for lessons, but Mrs Gait has given us all their elementary music books and Anna says she will come down and help you. And soon we might find somebody who can teach you, not too expensively . . ."

Lorna moved across to where her mother was sitting. Demonstrations of affection didn't come easily to her but she put her arms round her mother and kissed her.

"It's so lovely, Mum. It's so good of you and," the emotion which choked her voice made it difficult to complete the sentence, "I'm sorry about everything, Mum."

Mother and daughter hugged one another. "How did you manage to find the money?" Lorna asked a few minutes later.

Barbara Rawlinson found it important to take Lorna's clothes upstairs at that moment. Then she was preoccupied with making some lunch while her daughter tinkled happily on the piano. In Lorna's ever-active imagination it was just a short leap to the haunting, expressive music she had heard at the vicarage.

"But Mum," she persisted later, "how could you afford it?"

Eventually, in the face of Lorna's insistent questioning, Barbara Rawlinson admitted hesitantly that Doug had bought the piano. He had been looking for an inexpensive one ever since Lorna had first mentioned the subject. He had been so anxious to have it in place ready for her return home.

Lorna was touched. "It's terribly kind of him." She was keenly aware that she had not earned such generosity and anxious to make reparations for the damage she had done.

She began to work out what she could say to Doug, framing in her mind some words of thanks – and of apology.

But he did not visit that day. Or the next. Or even the next week.

"I expect he has other things to do." Mrs Rawlinson was evasive. She gave a half-smile. "You could send him a letter of thanks. I think that would be a nice thing to do."

No. She did not know when he would be coming round again. Lorna was suspicious. She was not easily deterred.

"All right," her mother eventually conceded. "Doug is not coming round again."

Lorna was ashamed of the momentary delight the news afforded. "He must come," she insisted, pushing her better instincts to the fore. "Is it because of me? Have you told him not to come?"

Mrs Rawlinson nodded unhappily.

"Oh Mum, I am sorry. Truly." It cost Lorna at lot to say those words. "Please ask him to come. Tell him I'm sorry."

"No. It's not a good idea."

"Please, Mum, please. I didn't mean to hurt you or him."

"No, Lorna, I can't take any more. I could never go through that again." Her mother was shaking slightly but there was a sharpness to her voice at the same time.

"Mum, it won't be the same again. You must see him if you want to."

"No." Lorna was startled by the frozen look on her mother's face.

"But why, Mum? Please." Lorna reached out for her mother's hand. Mrs Rawlinson stood quite still. When she spoke her voice sounded remote and detached.

"I'm not strong enough, Lorna, to oppose you, just as I wasn't strong enough to stand up to your father. Yes, I know he was a good man and a clever one. But he was also a very dominating, strong-willed person. Your father, your grandmother and you – you all want me to be something I'm not!"

Barbara Rawlinson lit herself a cigarette clumsily, her fingers fumbling over the matches.

"You are all so set in your ways and so sure you are right – the Rawlinsons are all the same." In her passion she seemed to have forgotten that only Lorna was left.

"You forced me to choose between you and Doug. You win. Every time. I love you, Lorna, and I loved your father. I realized when you were hurt that if anything happened to you, too, I think I should go out of my mind." Outwardly Mrs Rawlinson now seemed calm and controlled.

Lorna was shocked into silence. Then she sank into an armchair, put her hands to her face and wept. In an instant, her mother's arms were round her.

"It's not your fault, Lorna. It's the way you are. We'll go back to how it was before and forget the last few months." Lorna could hear the sad resignation in her mother's voice as they clung to one another.

Chapter Twenty-One

But it wasn't possible to wipe away the last few months. Not only was the piano a constant reminder of Doug, but Lorna was well aware that beneath her mother's cheerful manner there was a heaviness of spirit.

She had to persuade Doug to come to their house. A letter wasn't likely to work. She would have to talk to him personally, explain she was sorry . . .

Lorna wrote him a warm letter of thanks and decided to take it round to his house one Saturday morning. Her mother would think she was taking Patch out for a walk.

She knew Doug's address. He lived on a council estate at the other end of the town.

Lorna walked briskly. Gauntsford in the spring was a sad sight. The brightness of the sunlight accentuated the dark monotony of the streets of flat, terraced houses. Houses that were at least cosy against the blasts of winter cold put up equal defences against the warm sunlight. The sharp, clear light tried to find a little natural green life and discovering none, glared harshly on the scene.

Lorna passed the dominating hulk of the factory where her mother and Doug worked, then the Mechanics' Institute not much further along, adjacent to a bleak, bombed site.

Orchard Estate spread out in front of Lorna, a maze of houses, the roads trying to disguise their ordinariness by curving back on themselves. Finding 13, Willow Way was much harder than she had envisaged. Pine, Elm, Maple, Chestnut, Larch – each street was named after a different tree – and whichever avenue Lorna followed she seemed to come back to where she had started.

Two or three inquiries later she found the address for which she was looking. Nervously she stepped up the small front garden path and knocked on the door.

"Yes?" The tone was aggressive as Lorna faced the large, heavily-built older woman who answered the door in her apron. This must be Doug's mother.

"I'm Lorna Rawlinson," she said apprehensively. "I wondered if I could speak to Mr Meldrum?"

The woman eyed her curiously but did not seem inclined to be helpful.

"He's out." She was decisive and went to shut the door.

"I brought him a letter," Lorna interposed quickly. "Is Andrew there?"

"He is but he is not free right now." Mrs Meldrum left no room for discussion. She held out her hand to take the letter just as a car drove up to the door.

"You had better come in and sit down. I'll attend to you later." Her face had clouded at the sight of her visitors.

Lorna was guided into the front room. A couple got out of the car and followed her into the house. As Lorna entered the room she was startled by the sight of Andrew. For once he was immaculately dressed and did not need the dressing down with a clothes brush which his grandmother insisted on giving him. But it was his expression that horrified Lorna.

His face was drained of colour and utterly miserable. He visibly shrank from the woman who descended upon him. Lorna had only the haziest impression of a short fur coat and a mass of smooth black curls piled unnaturally high on top of the woman's head.

Everyone seemed oblivious of Lorna's presence. She had just time to wonder why this woman painted her lipstick in a bow right above her natural lip before the couple swept Andrew out of the house. The man, who had a small, clipped moustache, hovered in the background.

"You'll be sure to bring him back by seven." Mrs Meldrum's voice was authoritative and unfriendly. Only the briefest of civilities were entered into before the car drew swiftly away.

Chapter Twenty-Two

Mrs Meldrum went straight into the kitchen to fill up a kettle of water. She looked startled when Lorna followed her in. She seemed to have forgotten about the girl.

"I feel so angry whenever I see her. Painted arrogant hussy. Thinks of nobody but herself." She didn't seem inclined to inquire about the reason for Lorna's visit. She set out two tea cups and Lorna saw her visibly begin to thaw.

She guessed that Doug had made himself scarce to avoid meeting his former wife. But that expression on Andrew's face, that she would never forget.

"It's wicked what she has done to that boy," Mrs Meldrum went on. "And she always manages to look so pleased with herself."

Lorna sipped her tea.

"Could you give Doug – er, Mr Meldrum – this letter please? He works with my mother, Barbara."

"He's at work today. It's his weekend on – but I'll

give it him directly he gets home." The older woman showed no interest in the contents of the envelope and retreated again into her thoughts.

"Of course!" she said with sudden vehemence, "you're the silly girl who went chasing off in the middle of the night and fell down the steps."

Mrs Meldrum was clearly one of those people who deem it a virtue to speak their minds. There wasn't anything to say in reply. Lorna merely nodded.

"Well, we certainly could have done without that. We've problems enough without you adding to them. You gave Andrew a proper turn. Shaking like a leaf, he was, when he got home, poor little soul. As if he hadn't enough on his plate already with a mother like that. Always did put herself first. Unnatural, she is. I wouldn't let her see him at all, but Doug, he's so soft. Always gives in . . . And there was Andrew white as a sheet and shaking." Mrs Meldrum's thoughts darted hither and thither. "I wrapped him up in a blanket and gave him a nice cup of Horlicks. There's nothing better than a good hot drink when you've had a shock. Poor little soul."

She looked thoughtful. "He was a beautiful little lad with all that blond, curly hair. And so good. No trouble at all. Everyone used to admire him when he was out. Bright as a button too. He was doing so well at school till all that . . ." Mrs Meldrum paused to pick her words, "carry on. His mother never had any time for him when she got her fancy man. Now he doesn't do a thing at school. Doesn't try, poor little soul. And it's all her fault. Her going knocked the stuffing out of our Andrew. Doesn't try, that is what all his reports say. And it's true. It's the devil's own job to get him to take the right books to school. Let alone look after his clothes. He would wear two odd socks if you let him. Just switched off, he is. Unnatural, that's what she is. And her with such a lovely little boy. Unnatural.''

Mrs Meldrum turned her thoughts back to the present. ''And you haven't helped any.'' She looked directly at Lorna. ''Heaven knows what you might have done to your poor mother. Even my poor Doug hasn't been himself since that night. Quiet, he is, in himself again. It's hard to raise a laugh out of him. Just like he was before. And he was just beginning to get a bit of life back in him, too. Sometimes I think we must have had all our packet of bad luck. It's our turn for the good bit. But just when we seem to get to a better patch something else happens like this and back we are again to more trouble.''

Her indignation seemed to have run its course.

''Still, perhaps there is a reason we don't know,'' she mused. ''And it could have been a whole lot worse. You're lucky to be around – and looking so bright-eyed and bushy-tailed. I remember the last time it happened and she didn't live to tell the tale. Goodness knows why anyone should want to go out to such a lonely place in the middle of the night.''

''What did happen when Rosie fell down the steps?'' It was worth surviving the ticking off if Lorna could learn something to illuminate the scene that kept replaying through her mind.

''Rosie! She warn't called Rosie. Miss Veronica, it was.''

She poured herself another cup of tea non-committally. Lorna thought she wasn't going to continue. The kitchen clock ticked away in the silence. Then Mrs Meldrum began.

''Why she went out that night I'll never know. Don't suppose anyone ever will. The wind and the rain that night were something wicked. There I was in the kitchens wondering how I was to get home, and me with only a thin coat, and Miss Veronica went out without so much as a wrap. It was the sort of night when you had a feeling awful things might happen. I remember it clear as if it were yesterday. The wind seemed to blow the big trees right over the house. Any minute you thought they might crash in." She shuddered at the recollection.

"And what was she doing in the garden that night? Had she arranged to meet Mark?"

"So you know about *that*, do you? Well, she couldn't have seen him that evening, that I do know. I had been down to his house that very afternoon with a letter from her and he had already gone off to Liverpool, so his sister told me and I had no reason to doubt her.

"There we were, so busy in the kitchen making little tarts and piping fancy designs on the salmon for all those guests, but Miss Veronica was so insistent. I must take this letter for her. Mr Judd, he would have had a fit if he had known. It was more than my job was worth, make no mistake, but Miss Veronica was so upset. 'Please,' she said, 'take this for me. I'll not ask you to do anything for me ever again.' Not that she ever did, poor little soul."

"But did she know Mark had already left?"

"Couldn't say. I never did get a chance to talk to her again. We were so busy in the kitchens with all those guests. You've never seen food like it. And everything had to be done just so for Mr Judd. A better training than people get today, it was. None of your short cuts. There are people who call themselves cooks nowadays who can't make a Victoria sponge without it sinking, let alone a

Pavlova. Not that you get much practice with the rations we're allowed."

Lorna didn't want to know about cooking. "But what did happen that night?" she persisted.

"We'd just cleared the tables when the scullery girl came running in, shaking like a leaf. 'Miss Veronica,' she said, 'she's had a terrible accident. They've just carried her in.' It was dreadful. Mr Judd was in a panic, shouting that somebody must get the doctor. Mrs Judd was terrified. Couldn't do a thing. She never was one for coping. The guests just seemed to take themselves off. The village doctor came quickly but there wasn't much he could do. The next day Mr Judd sent for some big name doctor from London. He would spend any money, he said, if somebody could get his daughter right. But it wasn't any good. It was three days before she died. It were a terrible time. Her father were nearly out of his mind and her mother just sat crying all the while. They never did get over it, I'm told."

Lorna shuddered at the thought of what she might have done to her own mother.

"Miss Veronica was a lovely girl," Mrs Meldrum went on. "They do say that only the good die young. Old Mr Judd never did deserve a daughter like that. Any more that that woman deserves our Andrew." Mrs Meldum set about clearing up the cups.

"I used to have to walk six miles to work in those days," she recalled, leaping around in her thoughts in her characteristic way. "It were before six when I left home and I was never back till well after eight. Not that it did us any harm. When I think what we had to put up with compared with young people today, it makes me laugh." But Lorna noticed that she didn't sound much like laughing.

"But Mark and the money," Lorna persisted. "What do you think happened?"

"Money? What money?" Mrs Meldrum looked puzzled.

"The money Mark was accused of stealing."

"Oh that! There was talk of some money being missing. I never did give it much thought, to be honest. Mr Judd was beside himself after Miss Veronica died, trying to blame everybody for everything. I can't be sure. Not that it matters much now, does it? It's all so long, long ago, just water under the bridge. What I did learn in that big house is that money doesn't buy happiness. Miss Veronica had everything that money could buy. Such a lovely lass but, oh, she was lonely! On her own so much. There were never other young people in the house for her. She used to come into the kitchen and talk to me. She loved to hear me chat about my brothers and sisters. We may not have had much money but we did know how to have fun. I think in her way she envied me. 'Tell me more about Donald,' she would say. That was my young brother who was always getting into scrapes. Donald was the . . ."

"But Miss Veronica and Mark, did they meet much?"

"He was up at the big house every day. 'Make Mark a birthday cake,' Miss Veronica said one day. And I had to try to do it in the kitchen without anyone noticing. And that took some doing, I can tell you. A great one for presents, she was. She used to give me ribbons and silk petticoats that she didn't want any more. Miss Ronie, Mark always called her. Nobody else would have dared. But he had a cheeky way with him. You couldn't help but like him."

Ronie? Presents? The words leapt out from the

letter Veronica had sent to Mark, the letter in Gran's casket. Perhaps that was the one Mrs Meldrum had delivered to the cottage – too late. It all began to make sense to Lorna. That would explain why Gran still had the letter. The lady in blue had soil on her hands. She had been digging. She had left a present for Mark. But where? It would be like searching for a needle in a haystack in those wild grounds.

"Where you always find me," she repeated aloud the words in the letter. "Did they have a meeting place? Somewere they always saw one another?" Her voice was excited. The present must still be there. Mark had never returned to collect it. He might never have know Veronica had left it.

"Not any as I knew of. She would wander all over the grounds with him. Unless," said Mrs Meldrum reflectively, "it was by the lake. She always loved sitting there and I do know as he planted blue flowers all alongside specially for her. It was such a happy colour, she used to say. The colour of the sky on a bright sunny day."

The blue catkins. Somewhere by one of those plants near the lake was the gift Veronica had buried for Mark to take on his trip. Her last present to him. Lorna would study the drawings again. She had to find it even if the plant had long since died. That was what the blue lady in the field of flowers had been trying to tell her.

She could hardly wait to get back to the gardens.

Mrs Meldrum was starting to prepare vegetables.

"Funny the way history repeats itself," she said. "You falling down those same steps. One of Mark's family, too. You've the look of the Wolstenholmes. That thick hair and dark eyebrows."

History does repeat itself, thought Lorna guiltily.

More than Mrs Meldrum realized. And for the same reason. All because a man wasn't thought good enough for the family.

"Please," she appealed, "tell Doug I would like him to come to our house again. I'm sorry. Really sorry for causing you more trouble. And I'm so grateful for the piano. It's lovely."

"Well, I'll tell him what you said – but whether it will make any difference, that I wouldn't like to say." Mrs Meldrum shrugged her shoulders. "I don't know as you can turn the clock back."

Lorna found herself hoping fervently that she could turn it back – and unravel some of the past.

Chapter Twenty-Three

It was June. The war in Europe had ended. Families were exuberantly happy, but Lorna and her mother remained outside the general festivities. They had no one to welcome back and life for them went quietly on.

Doug had never reappeared at 102 Princess Street despite Lorna's plea. She had done well in her examinations even with the interruption to her schoolwork which the accident had caused. Long evenings meant she could now spend more and more time pushing her way through thickets that surrounded the lake.

Blue flowers there were in plenty, but wild. Tiny, bright-eyed plants spread round the edge of what had once been gardens. Forget-me-nots had strayed everywhere. But years of leaf droppings had covered the soil where Mark had laid out his plants and a prickly wilderness had taken hold.

It was a hopeless task to find the spot where Mark

and Veronica had held their trysts. Mark's plans revealed not a clue, even though Lorna pored over them hour after hour.

But she was nothing it not determined. She resolved to clear one patch of the gardens round the lake after another – even if it did take her years. She borrowed a spade and some cutting shears from Mr Dean.

She embarked on her task from a point just behind the cherub. It was back-breaking work. The spade would hardly penetrate the undergrowth and the stems of the invading shrubs were too thick for garden shears to cut. After all, they had had it all their own way for more than forty years.

It needed a saw to hack through the undergrowth. Lorna realized that she was simply not physically strong enough for this task: she still hadn't regained all her strength after the fall.

Determined nevertheless, she was wandering, dirty and dishevelled, over the village green with a handsaw borrowed from Mr Dean when she bumped into Andrew.

"What's going on?" he asked.

Disjointedly she told him about the search.

"Mind if I come too?" His voice was eager. Lorna was glad to have help. Andrew might be stronger than she was at sawing away the twisted branches.

She outlined the tale as they walked back to the lake.

"Where you always find me," Andrew repeated the phrase to himself several times.

"I know!" he said excitedly. "There's a plant called veronica. That must be it."

Lorna's heart leapt up – but only momentarily. "But there wasn't one on the plan," she said flatly. "I know the names off by heart."

"Well, there is," Andrew countered triumphantly. "That must be it. I'm pretty sure we have it in our garden. Look, let's go back to my house first and find out what it looks like."

Lorna knew her mother would be appalled at the idea of her calling on Doug's family, in her present grubby state, clutching a handsaw – but nothing could hold her back. She gave Patch a shout and together the three of them set off for the Orchard estate.

If Mrs Meldrum was surprised to see them she didn't show it.

"Dad's in the garden," she said, leading them outside. "He's the one that knows about plants."

Lorna felt self-conscious at meeting Doug for the first time since her fall. He stopped digging and came up to greet them warmly.

"Dad, what does veronica look like?" demanded Andrew.

"It's here along this bed," answered his father. Lorna recognized the little blue flower which had crept all over the edges of the lake gardens. Her heart sank. That gave no clue at all.

"It's no good," she explained. "That is everywhere. It's more of a bush or a tree I am looking for."

Andrew was thoughtful.

"I've got an idea there is another one," he said. "There are blue flowers on some of my stamps. Stay here."

He ran indoors, leaving Lorna alone with Doug.

"Everything all right at your house?"

Lorna nodded.

"The piano's marvellous. I love it," she told him. "I've learned my scales from Anna's books. Will you come round and hear them sometime? It will be ages before I can play anything good but I have been able to pick out a tune called Sweet Molly Malone."

Doug laughed but Lorna noticed that he didn't respond to her invitation.

"Come on in," Andrew was shouting from the house. Lorna found him clutching a pile of stamp albums.

"I've got two books here. I'm sure the flower stamps are in one," he said excitedly. "You go through this one. I'll do the other."

Lorna was impatient. This was pointless. She could not believe that this was the way to find the answer. She would rather be digging round the lake. Without enthusiasm she began thumbing through pages of stamps.

"Just look for blue flowers," Andrew directed, "and the name. Somebody," he mused, "came out with a whole set of blue flowers."

They sat for what seemed a long time working their way fruitlessly through the stamps. Mrs Meldrum brought them drinks of lemonade.

"Somewhere there is a veronica and it is not the same as the plants in our garden." Andrew would not stop to have his drink.

Lorna's attention was wandering when Andrew called out, "Veronica, hebe."

"Hebe, hebe. That *is* on the plan. And look, it has catkins too." Lorna bent over to examine the stamp.

"Dad, can you run us back to Lorna's house? It's important. Really important. Please!" Andrew had hared down the garden.

"I'll have to have a quick wash and tidy up," said Doug. But at least he didn't refuse. He combed his hair with care before they all, Patch included, climbed into his small car.

"Lorna, what's this?" Barbara Rawlinson was startled when they descended on her. She turned pale. For a second she thought there had been another accident. There was soil on Lorna's face and she had leaves in her hair.

"Everything's absolutely fine." Lorna didn't bother with any explanation. She rushed up to her room to find the plan.

"It's here. Come on," she called out to Andrew, "we'll take it back to the lake. Thanks for the lift," she added, turning to Doug.

"We'll be back later," she shouted to her mother as the three figures – Lorna, Andrew and Patch – rushed from the house.

"You must have a wash," Mrs Rawlinson called after her. But it was too late. They were gone.

She looked at Doug, mystified. "What's happening?"

He shrugged.

"Search me. But those two seem to have come to some sort of understanding."

Chapter Twenty-Four

Lorna was far more impatient than Andrew.

"Come on. It must be this way."

"No. It's not. You've got it wrong." He insisted on estimating the scale of the plan from the size of the lake, walking it out in strides. Then he laid the plan down on the terrace and was painstakingly slow in trying to calculate the precise position of the shrub. Eventually he was satisfied with the outcome of his reasoning.

"I'd guess it's about four feet in from the edge of the garden in this direction," he said, pointing to the right of the cherub.

"Oh, do hurry up!" Lorna had already set off in the direction he was indicating.

"We don't want to waste time hacking our way through this jungle if we are going in the wrong direction." There was a self-assurance about Andrew which surprised Lorna.

She realized as they pushed their way through

twisted branches and prickly, stinging weeds just how daunting their task would be. How could they ever identify one particular spot?

"You will have to saw away some of these branches and I'll do the heavy digging," instructed Andrew as they approached the area where he reckoned their work should start. "I should think the veronica was strangled long ago, so we will just have to dig where it would have been."

Both were soon covered with scratches and nettle stings. But they were equally determined.

"Look I'll hold this branch out of the way while you saw the other one. No, you don't saw like that!" Andrew had taken charge of the operation. "Hold it straight."

It took all of Andrew's strength to push a spade into the ground. The two worked away companionably but made very slow progress. Every so often the spade would hit something hard. There was a moment of anticipation before a large stone or piece of rubbish was uncovered. It was exhausting work which didn't leave much breath for talking.

"That dog," Andrew grumbled as Patch scampered through the undergrowth showering them for the hundredth time with old, dry leaves. The mongrel hadn't had so much fun in a long time.

Then he stopped frolicking and began to sniff intently, working purposefully as if he was trying to follow a trail. Lorna, bored by the seeming impossibility of their task, stopped work to pursue him on all fours, scrambling through the undergrowth.

It was when Patch stood still, sniffing very intently into the air, that she first caught sight of them. Blue catkins and grey-green leaves like fingers. "Here!" she shrieked to Andrew. "It's here, the veronica."

She heard the sound of brittle twigs snapping as he made his way towards her.

Momentarily she caught a glimpse of swaying cornflower blue as though a skirt were sweeping by. She had seen that nodding blue once before – and thought it was a shrub in bloom.

Lorna was suddenly struck with the sense of another presence by her side in the undergrowth. She stood transfixed. It was as though someone were trying to give her a message, wanting to say something imperative.

"Lorna! Where are you?" Andrew's irritated voice brought her back to reality. The momentary sensation was gone.

Lorna was on her hands and knees, digging with her fingers through the dead leaves. Patch, thinking it was game, joined in with his back legs while Andrew systematically broke off branches to give himself room to dig.

"Damn," muttered Lorna, shaking her hand after stubbing her fingers on something hard. She worked on with her bare hands furiously. There was a rigid surface under the earth. It was metal, for sure.

"Come and dig this out!"

Andrew was on the spot with the spade. "Mind out!" It wasn't long before the object was brought to the surface. A trowel. Both experienced a keen sense of anti-climax. Somebody must have left it in the garden.

"There was soil on Veronica's hands when she fell." The words replayed through Lorna's mind.

"She must have left the trowel to show him where to dig." A renewed sense of excitement welled up in Lorna.

Andrew nodded. He continued to dig patiently at

the spot. Every now and then he hit an obstacle – but it was just a stone or an old root. Willing him to succeed, Lorna was sure she was not alone: someone else was watching him too, urging him on.

Again the spade hit something. This time it was substantial. There was definitely something here. Lorna clawed away at the edges, breaking her nails, while Andrew tried to lever it up with the spade. Triumphantly they brought to the surface an old, rusty cash box.

"We've done it." Andrew's voice was excited. They smiled at each other, the confidential smile of friends who have accomplished something together, and carried the box on to the terrace.

The box was heavily rusted but not locked. It was Lorna who took the side of the trowel and gradually eased the sides apart. Andrew had subsided on to the terrace exhausted from all his digging.

Suddenly the lid sprang back. They both gasped. There they were. Still gleaming. A heap of golden guineas. "I was right. Mark never did take the money. It was here all the time." Lorna was exultant. Her triumph was not just for Mark, but for Gran and her father, too.

"It must be worth a fortune now," said Andrew slowly.

"We're rich," yelled Lorna, dancing round the terrace. "Andrew, think of all the things we can have!" The "we" sprang from her lips spontaneously and as she said it she realized in a flash of recognition that she might now have a real flesh-and-blood brother.

Delighted as he was with the find, Andrew kept his feet firmly on the ground.

"It is not ours," he insisted. "It must belong to the

people at the big house, wherever they are now. But," he added more optimistically, "there might be a reward for finding it. Come on. Let's pick up all the things and take it back to your place."

Both Lorna and Andrew now began to realize how tired they were. Just the thought of the walk home seemed an effort. As they gathered up their things Lorna looked up at Andrew. "Thank you," she said. "I would never have done it on my own." His face glowed with pleasure.

As they prepared to leave and Lorna turned round for one last look at the scene, something caught her eye.

"Look!" She grabbed Andrew's arm excitedly. "Do you see the blue gown behind that shrub?"

Andrew's gaze followed the direction in which she was pointing. "That is not a dress," he said prosaically. "That is a ceanothus bush."

Lorna heard the pride in his voice, the pride of someone who knows he has the right answer.

It never occurred to her to argue. She knew the truth.

Chapter Twenty-Five

Their feet dragged with tiredness as they trudged home, laden with garden tools and taking it in turns to clutch the precious money box. Only Patch still had the energy to race around.

"I could eat a horse," commented Andrew companionably.

"You've probably eaten quite a few already," joked Lorna. With all the wartime shortages of meat there were always stories in circulation of butchers selling horsemeat.

Andrew shuddered. "Don't!"

"Perhaps with all this money I can have music lessons," suggested Lorna. "That is – if we do get a reward. You never know, they might never trace the owners. What do you want to do with your half?"

Andrew looked gratified at the suggestion that he was an equal partner.

"I don't know," he mused. "I suppose I would like a proper holiday, somewhere by the sea. I have never been to the seaside. Or," he added, turning his thoughts closer to home, "we could spend it all on chocolate bars, tins of condensed milk and lots of treacle. I can never think why grown-ups eat anything else."

"What I would like most," considered Lorna in a more serious mood, "would be a new home, somewhere pretty, with flowers in the front garden and fields you could look out on." There was a house just like that which she always passed on her way to school.

"There is not enough money for that," commented Andrew sensibly, "even if we could keep it all."

They had reached 102 Princess Street and banged hard with the knocker.

Mrs Rawlinson looked bright-eyed and flustered when she opened the door.

"Lorna! Andrew! Goodness, how dirty you look, and there is someone to see you. Come on. We will have to do something with these." She took hold of the garden implements. "What a day it has been. And you will never guess who is here."

Patch bounded up to a tall, upright, white-haired man who had risen to his feet. He smiled and Lorna was struck by the whiteness of his teeth against his sunburnt skin. There was something familiar about those dark, penetrating eyes and heavy eyebrows but for the moment she could not place it. Momentarily she forgot about their find.

"Know who I am?" He grinned. His voice had an accent – but which? "I'm here just because of you," he explained.

Lorna was thrown into confusion. "Not a doctor about the accident?"

He shook his head. "I haven't heard about that."

"A policeman?" She had a horrible thought. Perhaps they had no right to dig up the money. Maybe someone had been watching them from a distance. Someone hostile.

Again he shook his head.

She stared from him to her mother and then Doug. All were smiling. Nothing must be wrong. She looked at the visitor intently and the truth came to her in a flash.

"Mark!" The eyes, they were the same as Gran's.

"But," she stammered, "the money. We've just found the money. Andrew and me. Andrew – this is my great uncle Mark. The man in charge of those gardens, who drew the plans. The money was meant for him. Look!" She exclaimed, throwing open the box.

"Lorna! What have you been doing? Where did you get this?" Mrs Rawlinson was agitated. "And what are these branches dropping leaves on the carpet?"

"Veronica," said Mark as Lorna's mother swept away the twigs of the shrub which Andrew and Lorna had tried to dislodge. "I was going to wander up to the lake tomorrow but you have beaten me to it. I got your letter, Lorna, thanks. I guessed that something must be hidden by the veronica but I didn't fancy my chances of finding it now. So there really was money missing. I guess I thought it was a trick by the old man to discredit me."

"You really do still live at Rafferty Falls then?"

"No, I didn't stay there more than a year or two. But not long back I ran up against the fellow who still runs the post office there. We had a chat about old times and what had happened to us since. He went to a lot of trouble to trace my present address when your letter arrived. Good job that Wolstenholme is an unusual name."

"But Lorna, Andrew, I want to know about this money?" Mrs Rawlinson was still uneasy.

"We worked out where it was and dug it up." There was pride in Andrew's voice, his eyes bright with pleasure.

Gradually, piece by piece, the story came out.

"Well, we'll have to take these guineas up to the police station tomorrow," said Mark decisively. "They will have to trace whoever inherited the estate."

"But they are probably rich anyway. They won't notice the difference." Lorna could not suppress a feeling of disappointment. "And Veronica wanted you to have the money."

"I wouldn't take a penny from the Judds." There was a cold decisiveness in Mark's voice. "I managed very well without their help. I have made more than enough for my family."

"Family? You married someone else? But Veronica – she went out in the storm to give it to you." Things were not working out as Lorna had dreamed. "She died." Her voice cracked.

"Oh yes, I married." Mark looked surprised at the undisguised shock in Lorna's voice. "This all happened more than half a lifetime ago," he added more gently. "It did take me a very long time to get over the shock of Ronie's death. It was all so sad, so unfinished . . . But everything changes. Life goes on."

Lorna looked uncertain.

Mark smiled. "You look so like Emily," he said. "That serious look. I'd have known that face anywhere. I did wander up to the village church this afternoon." His face was solemn. "I looked at her grave. Dear Emily. She was a good sister, so kind and conscientious. I did often think of coming home but there were the children to put through college and then the war came. It's a pity . . ." His voice trailed off. "And I never was anything of a writer. But look, you're probably all wanting your tea and I have to get back to the railway station. I've left my case there. Then I'll have to find a bed for the night."

"You must stay here," Mrs Rawlinson said quickly. "Lorna can come in with me."

"I'll run you to the railway station," offered Doug. "We'll bring your luggage back. Then Andrew and I had best be making tracks. My mother will be wondering where we've got to."

"You know Andrew's grandmother," Lorna informed Mark. "Mrs Meldrum from the kitchens at the big house."

Mark shook his head. "I don't remember. I'm dreadful at names and it gets worse as I get older. I do recall one little girl, tiny, bright little thing like a sparrow. Then there was a capable, stand-no-nonsense girl who liked to take charge and was a marvellous hand at the cakes and puddings. Now, what was her name?" He puckered his brow.

"Elsie?" suggested Doug smiling. "That sounds like my mother."

"That's it. Elsie." Mark's face lit up with the recognition. "My, that girl could chat. But she had a kind heart."

"Still the same," commented Doug. Andrew nodded in agreement. "Right, we'll have to get weaving. There's the railway station to go to, then Mr Dean's to drop off Patch and the tools. Then it's home."

"Not George Dean next to Emily?" Mark asked. Doug nodded.

"Fancy, George Dean still there," Mark ruminated. "He used to think the world of Emily when they were young. But he never did pluck up courage to ask her out. Look, I've an idea. Let's all get together and have a bit of a party tonight. I'll go up to the Railway Tavern – if it is still there – and see if I can get a few bottles. You bring your mother," he nodded towards Doug, "and we'll ask George Dean, that is as long as you don't mind giving him a lift. And we'll have a grand reunion."

Mrs Rawlinson's eyes were alight. "I'd love that. It would be such fun. You will come, won't you?" she asked Doug and Andrew.

Doug nodded. "It sounds great."

Even Andrew looked pleased at the prospect. "I'll see you later," he said to Lorna. She had never seen him look happier.

"Fine," replied Lorna. She and Andrew now had a bond.

Chapter Twenty-Six

Everyone had been found somewhere to sit in the front room at 102 Princess Street. Chairs from bedrooms had been squeezed into every available space. Lorna, squatting on the floor, felt engulfed in the warm familiarity of a family gathering, something she had hardly known before.

Mark was making sure that everyone's glass was topped up. He had brought a large bunch of flowers for Barbara Rawlinson. Now he was chatting easily to Doug. He seemed to like people.

"And what's been happening to you?" Elsie Meldrum demanded of the visitor from Canada. "I suppose you have made your fortune?"

"Well, we do have our own farm, a biggish place, and I must admit it's doing well," Mark answered. "It has been a long haul and hard work. But it's a good life. And now one of the boys has come in with me. I was pleased about that." There was pride in his voice.

"And your wife?" Lorna inquired tentatively.

"Oh, she can run the place as well as I do," explained Mark. "Margaret always was a country girl. Born on a farm. I don't suppose for a minute I would have got going if it hadn't been for her. She could turn her hand to anything on the farm – not that she does as much now. But when the children were little the two of us had to work round the clock. We didn't have any help in those days."

"I couldn't see Miss Veronica coping like that." Mrs Meldrum voiced aloud the thought that was passing through Lorna's mind.

"Yes. Many's the time that has crossed my mind," commented Mark. "But then of course she was never planning to follow me. The letter, the one I got just before I left, made that very clear. Said she would not see me again and that it would never work out. We came from different worlds, she said. That really hurt. I was dismissed good and proper. First by the father and then by the daughter."

"But she was going to come. Definitely," Lorna interposed. "I can prove it."

She ran upstairs and brought down Veronica's letter along with the snippets of material. Mark handled the fabric and stared hard at the message.

"That blue!" said Mrs Rawlinson looking on, "it's uncanny. It is almost the same colour as the dress I made for you. And the same steps." She shivered though the night was warm. "I don't think I'll make anything in blue ever again." She was still haunted by the thought of what might have happened that dreadful night.

Every now and then a cold sensation would grip her at the recollection of Lorna's still white face as she was carried home.

"It just doesn't add up," Mark was saying. "This letter says the exact opposite to the one I received before I left home. Emily wrote to me all about the accident and the missing money – but she never mentioned another letter. Perhaps she thought it would upset me all the more if I thought Ronie had intended to come. She insisted I mustn't write in case the police traced me. She didn't want to know my address. Straight as a die she was, wouldn't tell a lie."

"Mrs Meldrum took that letter round to Gran's," Lorna explained. "But you had already left for Liverpool."

"You mean that's the letter." Mrs Meldrum suddenly latched on to the conversation. "My goodness, Miss Veronica didn't know what she was asking. There we were up to our eyes in it in the kitchen and Mr Judd always on the warpath, it was more than my job was worth –"

Lorna's thoughts drew away. She had heard all this before. She caught Andrew's eyes and he gave her a knowing look.

"We didn't have any of this fancy equipment they have nowadays. We did everything the hard way. Mind you, it was a better way to learn. And there I was, in the middle of it all, having to walk down to the village with a letter you never got."

Mrs Meldrum seemed to relive her indignation afresh each time she remembered the incident. She viewed the episode, Lorna noticed, entirely from her own perspective.

Poor Veronica, Lorna thought. Did anybody look at things from her point of view?

"It was the butler who arrived with the letter saying we couldn't meet again," Mark recollected.

"I'm not surprised," said Mrs Meldrum. "He

didn't have to slip out furtively like I did, did he? I wouldn't be surprised if Mr Judd sent him down in the carriage. He wasn't the sort to risk his neck for anybody. Frank . . . somebody, he was called. Looked after himself, he did. My goodness, my mother would have had a fit if she had known what I did. She needed my money, what with my father being dead. You were glad to have a job – any job – in those days."

"You mean, Mr Judd had a hand in the letter I got?" Mark was beginning to piece together the events that had occurred just before he left.

"Well, old Mr Judd had made her write that letter, hadn't he? Stood over her while she copied it out. Miss Veronica was in tears about it. She sat in the kitchen, sobbing her heart out, she did. She had to write to you again. It had to be that afternoon. Guests or no guests."

Mrs Meldrum was an essentially good-hearted woman, but she was stronger on practicalities than on romance, Lorna observed.

A picture of the girl in blue flashed before Lorna's eyes. She saw the steps by the lake, the pool itself, the catkins and the figure of the girl being carried away. Did all that emotion, that caring and that pain, not count for anything now? She puzzled over the sense of it all.

True, Mark had told them that he had called his daughter Veronica, but he seemed happy enough with his present life.

Lorna's thoughts switched to her father. She saw him standing alongside her on the moorland. She saw the sun shining through the red-gold leaves that sad, sunny November day . . .

Then she was back at the happy, laughing gathering

at Princess Street. Did those two missing figures not have any part to play here any more?

Suddenly the answer came to her. It is because of them that we are here now, she told herself fiercely. It was Veronica's gift which had reunited the family. She was here now. And her father, too, Lorna realized. They were in their minds, alive in their memories.

She found the thought deeply reassuring. It gave a meaning to the very different tragedies.

Veronica had loved Mark and Lorna felt sure that she would not have wanted him to grieve for ever. It was good that the mystery was cleared up, that Mark was back here with the people who belonged to his past life and the two strands could now be woven together again. Perhaps that was what Veronica had wanted when she beckoned Lorna that night . . .

Mrs Rawlinson put her head back on her chair contentedly. She felt cocooned with happiness. She so liked having people around and they all seemed to be enjoying themselves. The Rawlinsons and the Meldrums. They mixed well, her old life and maybe the new. For the first time in months she felt a sense of optimism. She was at peace.

Even Lorna and Andrew seemed to have found something to draw them together. It was a joy to see her daughter so much a part of the gathering, so relaxed and at ease.

"Lorna. Do you think we could have a tune?" Doug's voice was tentative. He had learned the force of her refusals.

"I'm not very good," she stammered. "I only know a few scales and a couple of songs."

"Well, that is more than any of us," Mark contributed encouragingly. "Nobody here is in any mood to criticize. Let's have something we can sing."

Self-consciously Lorna made her way over to the piano. She succeeded in playing "Sweet Lass of Richmond Hill" with only a few mistakes. Everyone joined in – mostly out of tune, with Mr Dean adding a rumbly bass line.

Lorna had not chosen the song with any forethought – she knew too few to have a choice. But as she embarked on the tune once more, for the demanded encore, she thought to herself that the song's lass might be Veronica. A different girl, a different hill. But perhaps that was the best way to remember the girl in blue – in a chorus of happy voices.

HAUNTINGS by Hippo Books is a new series of excellent ghost stories for older readers.

Ghost Abbey by Robert Westall
When Maggie and her family move into a run-down old abbey, they begin to notice some very strange things going on in the rambling old building. Is there any truth in the rumour that the abbey is haunted?

Don't Go Near the Water by Carolyn Sloan
Brendan knew instinctively that he shouldn't go near Blackwater Lake. Especially that summer, when the water level was so low. But what was the dark secret that lurked in the depths of the lake?

Voices by Joan Aiken
Julia had been told by people in the village that Harkin House was haunted. And ever since moving in to the house for the summer, she'd been troubled by violent dreams. What had happened in the old house's turbulent past?

The Nightmare Man by Tessa Krailing
Alex first sees the man of his darkest dreams at Stackfield Pond. And soon afterwards he and his family move in to the old house near the pond — End House — and the nightmare man becomes more than just a dream.

A Wish at the Baby's Grave by Angela Bull
Desperate for some money, Cathy makes a wish for some at the baby's grave in the local cemetery. Straight afterwards, she finds a job at an old bakery. But there's something very strange about the bakery and the two Germans who work there. . .

The Bone-Dog by Susan Price
Susan can hardly believe her eyes when her uncle Bryan makes her a pet out of an old fox-fur, a bone and some drops of blood — and then brings it to life. It's wonderful to have a pet which follows her every command — until the bone-dog starts to obey even her unconscious thoughts. . .

All on a Winter's Day by Lisa Taylor
Lucy and Hugh wake up suddenly one wintry morning to find everything's changed — their mother's disappeared, the house is different, and there are two ghostly children and their evil-looking aunt in the house. What has happened?

The Old Man on a Horse by Robert Westall
Tobias couldn't understand what was happening. His parents and little sister had gone to Stonehenge with the hippies, and his father was arrested. Then his mother disappeared. But while sheltering with his sister in a barn, he finds a statue of an old man on a horse, and Tobias and Greta find themselves transported to the time of the Civil War. . .

The Rain Ghost by Garry Kilworth
What is the secret of the old, rusty dagger Steve finds while on a school expedition? As soon as he brings it home, the ancient-looking knife is connected with all sorts of strange happenings. And one night Steve sees a shadowy, misty figure standing in the pouring rain, watching the house . . .

The Haunting of Sophie Bartholomew by Elizabeth Lindsay
Sophie hates the house she and her mother have moved to in Castle Street. It's cold and dark and very frightening. And when Sophie hears that it's supposed to be haunted, she decides to investigate . . .

Picking Up the Threads by Ian Strachan
There's something strange going on at the rambling old house where Nicky is spending her holidays with her great-aunt. In the middle of the night, Nicky is woken up by the sound of someone crying for help. But when she goes to investigate, there's nobody there!

The Wooden Gun by Elizabeth Beresford
Kate is very unhappy on the Channel Island where she's spending her summer holidays. She senses a mysterious, forbidding atnosphere, but no one else seems to notice it. Is it just her imagination, or does the beautiful, sun-drenched island hide a dark secret?

The Devil's Cauldron by David Wiseman
Although Clare is blind, she lives her life to the full, and is never afraid of taking chances. So when she is told about the old smuggler's cave, she persuades her friend Ned to come with her to explore it. But the cave holds more than just memories of the violence it saw many years ago . . .

HIPPO CLASSICS

HIPPO CLASSICS is a series of some of the best-loved books for children.

Black Beauty by Anna Sewell £1.50
Black Beauty is a magnificent horse: sweet-tempered, strong and courageous, coloured bright black with one white foot and a white star on his forehead. His adventures during his long and exciting life make one of the most-loved animal stories ever written.

Alice's Adventures in Wonderland
by Lewis Carroll £1.50
When Alice sees the White Rabbit scurry by, her curiosity gets the better of her and she follows him down a rabbit hole. Suddenly she finds herself in an extraordinary world of mad tea parties, grinning Cheshire cats, lobster quadrilles and many more wonderful scenes and characters.

Wind in the Willows by Kenneth Grahame £1.50
One spring day Mole burrows out of the ground and makes his way to the river. There he meets Water Rat and is introduced to all Ratty's friends – Badger, Otter and the loveable and conceited Toad. There's an adventure-filled year ahead for all the animals in this classic story.

Kidnapped by R L Stevenson £1.50
David Balfour is cheated of his rightful estate and then brutally kidnapped. He manages to escape – but is forced to go on the run again when he's wrongfully accused of murder. An action-packed tale of treachery and danger.

The Railway Children by E Nesbit £1.50
The lives of Roberta, Peter and Phyllis are changed completely after the dreadful evening when their father is taken away. They move to the country, where they miss their friends and parties and trips to the zoo. Then they discover the nearby railway, and soon the children find their days filled with adventure.

Heidi by Johanna Spyri £1.50

An orphan, Heidi is left with her old grandfather who lives high in the mountains. Heidi soon learns to love her life with the kindly old man, the mountains, the goats, Peter the goat boy, and the people of the village. Then one day she is taken away to Frankfurt, and has to leave her friends far behind . . .

The Hound of the Baskervilles
by Arthur Conan Doyle £1.50

The Baskerville Curse has laid its deadly finger on every member of the family for hundreds of years. When the new heir, Sir Henry, arrives from Canada to claim his inheritance, he asks Sherlock Holmes for his help against the dreadful curse. And with his good friend Dr Watson, Holmes becomes embroiled in one of the most thrilling investigations of his career.

Treasure Island by R L Stevenson £1.50

When Jim Hawkins opens up Captain Flint's old sea chest, he is amazed to find a treasure map inside it. This discovery plunges him into a series of extraordinary adventures involving pirates, shipwreck, mutiny and murder, on his long and dangerous search for the island and its treasure.

A Christmas Carol by Charles Dickens £1.50

It's Christmas Eve, and as usual Scrooge is hard at work in his counting house, sneering at the good cheer and charitable spirit of people celebrating the festive season. But then the mean old man is visited by the Ghosts of Christmas Past, Christmas Present and Christmas Yet to Come, and he undergoes an amazing transformation.

Little Women by L M Alcott £1.50

Times are hard for the March sisters, with their father away at war and the family's lack of money. But the girls – Meg, Jo, Beth and Amy – let their enthusiasm and good nature shine through their troubles, and bring gaiety and hope to their own lives and those of the people around them.

White Fang by Jack London £1.50

In the frozen wastelands of north-west Canada, White Fang is born. Half-wolf, half-dog, he is the strongest and only survivor of the litter. And his strength and ferocity is put to the test again and again in this savage world where men and animals alike fight for survival.

Robinson Crusoe by Daniel Defoe £1.50

Shipwrecked on an uninhabited island, Robinson Crusoe has little hope of rescue or survival. But little by little he builds up a home for himself on the island. And then, after twelve years of solitude, he discovers footprints in the sand . . .

You'll find all these, and many more Hippo books, at your local bookseller, or you can order them direct. Just send off to *Customer Services, Hippo Books, Westfield Road, Southam, Leamington Spa, Warwickshire CV33 0JH*, not forgetting to enclose a cheque or postal order for the price of the book(s) plus 30p per book for postage and packing.

MARLENE MARLOWE INVESTIGATES

My name is Marlene. Marlene Marlowe. And I'm the
dottiest detective ever to have missed a clue . . .

Follow the hilarious trail of the world's most clueless
private eye in these books by Hippo:

Marlene Marlowe Investigates the Great Christmas
Pudding Mystery   £1.75
Early one morning Marlene is woken by a phonecall:
"Come to Peregrine Postlethwaite's bakery immediately!"
In the dimly-lit building Marlene follows a trail of dark red
sticky mess, leading to a large moving bundle . . .

Marlene Marlowe Investigates the Missing Tapes
Affair   £1.75
A phonecall summons Marlene to the house of an old
friend. There, slumped on the kitchen floor, lies the
twisted body of a young man . . .

You'll find these and many more great Hippo books at
your local bookseller, or you can order them direct. Just
send off to *Customer Services, Hippo Books, Westfield*
Road, Southam, Leamington Spa, Warwickshire CV33
OJH, not forgetting to enclose a cheque or postal order
for the price of the book(s) plus 30p per book for postage
and packing.

THE MALL

Six teenagers, all from different backgrounds, with one thing in common – they all want jobs at the new shopping Mall opening in Monk's Way. But working at the Mall brings rather more than most of them had bargained for . . .

Book 1: Setting Up Shop

Book 2: Open for Business

The new shopping Mall is opening soon, and the six teenagers who work there are already having problems. Ian is fired from his job at Harmony Records because of his dad's interference. Amanda's trying to fend of Mr Grozzi's advances at the restaurant. Jake's trying to hold down two jobs at once. And Simon's temper is threatening to cost him his job at the furniture store. Will life at the Mall prove too tough to handle?.

Book 3: Gangs, Ghosts and Gypsies

Problems are getting worse for the six teenagers who work part-time at the new shopping Mall. Simon's in trouble again, and this time it's cost him his job. Karen's having difficulties with her family. Goods are starting to disappear from the toy shop where Jake works. And there's a rumour going round that the Mall is supposed to be haunted!

Book 4: Money Matters

There are clashes at work and at home for the Mall kids. Ian and Kathy suspect that their boss at the record shop is involved in some shady deals. Simon's in the remand home, and won't tell the truth for fear of splitting on his friends. And Jake has a confession to make to the owners of the toy shop . . .

THE STEPSISTERS

When Paige's Dad marries Virginia Guthrie from Atlanta, she's thrilled that he's found someone to make him happy. But how will she get on with her new stepbrother and stepsisters? Especially Katie, the beautiful blonde fifteen-year-old, who looks like a model and can charm her way out of anything!

1   The War Between the Sisters   £1.75

Not only does Paige have to share her room with her stepsister, Katie, but then she finds that Jake, the boy she's fallen in love with, finds Katie totally irresistible. Paige's jealousy leads her to do some pretty stupid things to get her own back . . .

2   The Sister Trap   £1.75

Paige is delighted when she gets a job working on the school magazine. Especially when she becomes friendly with the magazine editor, Ben. But her jealousies over her beautiful stepsister, Katie, flare up again when Ben starts taking a lot of interest in Katie's swimming career.

3   Bad Sisters   £1.75

There's a rumour going round that Mike Lynch, the swimming champion, is cheating at school to stay on the team. And when Paige investigates the story for the school newspaper, she suspects that her stepsister, Katie, might be helping him. Should she find out the truth, even if it means getting Katie into trouble?

4   Sisters in Charge   £1.75

Paige is horrified when her dad and new stepmother announce they're going away together for a week. It means that she and Katie, her glamorous, popular stepsister, will be on their own together for the first time. Taking their past difficulties into account, Paige knows it won't be easy. But things turn out even more traumatic than either stepsister had suspected!